Hole in One

Hole in One

CATHERINE AIRD

St. Martin's Minotaur ❦ New York

www.minotaurbooks.com

ISBN 0-312-34229-2
EAN 978-0-312-34229-6

First published in Great Britain by Allison & Busby Limited

First U.S. Edition: August 2005

10 9 8 7 6 5 4 3 2 1

CATHERINE AIRD is the author of more than twenty crime novels and story collections, most of which feature Detective Chief Inspector CD Sloan. She holds an honorary M.A from the University of Kent and was made an MBE. Her other works include Amendment of Life and Little Knell. She lives in England.

Apart from writing the successful *Chronicles Of Calleshire* she has also written and edited a series of village histories and is active in village life.

Also by Catherine Aird

For Rachel and Douglas with love

The plot is based on the Old Testament story in the 2nd Book of Kings, Chapter Five, verses 1 – 27.

'Are they safe now?' asked Helen Ewell anxiously.

Ursula Millward peered forward, shading her eyes against the sun with her hand. 'Quite safe, I should say.'

'Are you sure?'

'I don't know how far you can hit,' responded Ursula with spirit, 'but they're well out of my range already.'

'That's a relief,' said Helen. She turned to face her friend. 'Do I go first or do you?' Both women were standing beside their trolleys on the first tee of the Berebury Golf Club.

Ursula Millward put both her hands out of sight behind her back. 'Which is it in? Right or left?'

'Left,' said Helen Ewell at once.

The other player brought her hands back into view and opened them. There was a golf tee in the left one. 'All right, you go first, then.' Ursula knew she should have said 'Your honour' but it still sounded funny to her. And anyway honour wasn't a word that came easily to mind when talking to Helen.

Helen Ewell carefully selected a number-two wood club from her golf bag, pressed a brightly coloured plastic tee into the ground, and placed her ball on it. Taking a deep breath she started to address it. After taking a couple of practice swings she stopped, grounded her driver and said again, 'You're quite sure I shan't hit them, Ursula, aren't you?'

'Quite sure,' said Ursula firmly.

She was right to be sure. Helen Ewell needn't have worried at all about her drive from the first tee hitting the players ahead. Even though she managed to hit the ball at her first attempt, she did so with such a wild swing that she topped it badly. Her ball did no more than trickle off the tee and on to the fairway in front of it.

'I'll never ever get it right,' she wailed. 'Ever, ever, ever...'

'Bad luck,' said Ursula immediately.

She herself managed a rather better shot and knocked her ball nearly a hundred yards down the fairway of the first hole.

Ursula Millward might be the better player of the two but she certainly wasn't the better dressed of the pair. From her stylish Tam O'Shanter headgear down to her elegant brown and white golf shoes, via a check shirt and shorts of exactly the right colour and length, Helen Ewell was perfectly accoutred for the game of golf. The fact that she could scarcely play the game was not nearly so important to her as looking the part.

'But,' Helen was still protesting, 'after my last lesson Jock told me I was really beginning to get a good grasp of my swing.'

'It'll come,' said Ursula Millward laconically. She refrained from remarking that all she had seen from the sidelines was the Golf Club professional, Jock Selkirk, getting quite a good grasp of Helen herself while trying to teach her that very same swing.

'Jock said that it's the way you take the club back that really matters,' said Helen. Her series of golf lessons from the Club's professional had come well after she'd made her many purchases in Berebury's best fashion shops, to say nothing of those carefully colour-coded items she'd bought in the pro's own shop beside the Clubhouse. Even the numbered covers on her wooden clubs matched the muted shades of her outfit.

'I can well believe it,' said Ursula dryly. She had also noticed that it had been while the golf professional's pupil had been taking a practice backswing that her friend had appeared to be in most need of the man's assistance. 'I expect,' she added a trifle maliciously, 'he thought the back swing was where he could be most helpful.'

'Oh,' agreed Helen eagerly. 'It is.'

'What Jock told me,' said Ursula, her tongue still well in

her cheek, 'was that getting your golf swing right in the first place is just like learning to ride a bicycle.'

'I'm sure he's right,' said Helen Ewell prettily, 'although it's something I could never do. Ride a bicycle, I mean.'

'That's the funny thing about golf – one day you can't hit a thing,' mused Ursula, half to herself, 'and suddenly the next day you can.' When she herself had first taken up the game she had only been able to afford a very short series of lessons from the professional at the Club, Jock Selkirk, but in any case she hadn't relished being pawed by the man.

'It's all very well for some,' said Helen petulantly. 'You seem to have picked it up all right, Ursula. Look at where your ball's got to...'

'Nevertheless,' rejoined Ursula Millward sturdily, 'there's no getting away from the fact that we're both still Rabbits.'

'I'm not sure that I want to win the Rabbits' Cup anyway,' sniffed Helen after she'd hit her ball again but not very far, this time with a number-five iron club.

'I don't think that winning is something we need to worry about,' said Ursula, well aware that her own second shot had not gone anything like as far as her first. 'Either of us.'

'You know, Ursula, I play so well when Jock is coaching me.' Helen slung her club back into her golf bag in manifest disappointment. 'It's not fair.'

Her friend forbore to remark that Helen performed everything better when there was a man – any man – watching her.

Instead she glanced over her shoulder and said 'I think we'd better keep going. There are some more Rabbits coming along behind and we don't want to have to let them play through us, do we?'

This was something that Helen and Ursula might not have wanted but in the event they had no option. In spite of the pair of them hurrying after their balls and playing as speedily as they could, the couple playing behind them kept gaining on them. On the second hole they were driving off the tee before Helen and Ursula had even reached the green; on the third hole they had to linger behind while Helen took four putts before she sank her ball.

'It's no good, Ursula,' Helen said in despair halfway down the fourth hole. 'I just can't play my best while they're just standing there waiting and waiting.'

'It is a bit unnerving,' admitted Ursula, 'being watched like this while we try to play.'

'I'd no idea that competitions were so nerve-racking,' moaned Helen as they panted up to the fifth tee.

Ursula grinned. 'You wait till we get to play in the Sharks versus the Minnows tournament.'

Helen made a face. 'I won't do it.' She glanced over her shoulder. 'Look, the others are holing out on the fourth already…it's not fair.'

'We'll wave them through on the sixth, shall we?' suggested Ursula, adding by way of consolation, 'They're much better than we are, anyway.'

'Good idea.' Helen readily assented to this. She shuddered. 'I couldn't bear it if they shouted "fore" at us.'

'Besides,' said Ursula looking about her appreciatively, 'it's a lovely day and the course is looking beautiful.'

This was true. The Berebury Golf Course had been carefully constructed round a mound – hardly a hill – just outside the town known as The Bield because of the wooden shelter on top of it. The name of the architect of the course was not known by the members, although the words "James Braid" were sometimes mentioned in passing – but without great conviction. It is more likely that the course hadn't had a proper architect at all, the holes having been created more by the lie of the land than by the hand of man.

Round one side of the Bield trickled a little stream. This configuration gave variety to the holes, some uphill and some down. From the highest tee of all there was a splendid view of the market town of Berebury. Better still, not even on a clear day could the factories of the distant industrial town of Luston be seen intruding on the pleasant landscape.

It was thus no hardship to Ursula Millward to stand aside to let the other players overtake them. The pair behind them were young women, too, but slightly older and playing a much steadier game. They accepted the invitation to play through Helen and Ursula with a gesture of thanks and hit their balls down the sixth fairway ahead of them noticeably farther than the other two had done.

'If,' remarked the one called Anna scornfully, 'those two are Rabbits, Christine, then I reckon we're practically hares.'

'Speak for yourself…blast!' The head of the other woman came up with a jerk after she'd taken her shot. 'Look! I think my ball's finished up in that awful bunker.'

'Not the big one at the back, I hope,' said Anna, peering ahead. 'You won't like that, I can tell you.'

Christine shoved her club back into her golf bag with quite unnecessary force.

'No, not that one, thank goodness. It's in the one to the right of the green. The shallow one, near the front.'

'That's not so bad then,' her companion reassured her. 'Colin says the men call the one at the back "Hell's Bells" because if you get in it, you can't get out…'

'Like Hell itself, I suppose,' said Christine soberly.

'And it ruins your card early on,' said Anna, ignoring this. The game of golf did seem to have a theology all of its own but she was still unsure what it was. 'Mind you,' she added judiciously, having already learned a little about the game, 'you'd have to have over-hit in a big way to go over the back there and into it. It's an enormous green and the slope's all in your favour.'

'David always says the sixth is the most difficult hole on the course anyway,' said her friend. 'And that I'd find that out for myself as soon as I started playing here at Berebury...'

Both women had announced that they were taking up the game purely in order to see more of their husbands. What they had neither admitted to aloud was that they were also doing so to make quite sure that some of the other lady players didn't see even more of those same husbands than they did.

Although Christine's ball was indeed in the shallower bunker – the one in front of the approach to the green – playing it out didn't present too many problems to her and both women holed out with quite a respectable score for a couple of tyros at the notorious sixth hole.

'I think playing the game does beat golf widowhood,' grinned Anna as she picked her ball out of the hole, 'but only just.'

'And only in good weather,' said Christine, scribbling on her card.

'Remember, we shan't be Rabbits for ever, either.' Anna had had one really good shot already. This had sent a quite unexpected frisson of delight through her lithe figure. Something quite poetic about the marriage of club, mind and body flitted through her mind and was gone, unexpressed and unformulated, but it had been there and she had registered the feeling of real pleasure in the game for the very first time.

'I'm not so sure about the pair behind us not staying as Rabbits for ever,' said Christine looking over her shoulder. 'Look, they've scarcely teed off yet and it's ages since we passed them.'

'Don't forget that fable about the hare and the tortoise,' Anna adjured her as they moved off towards the seventh tee. She wasn't at all sure she could repeat the one perfect shot she'd just had.

'Our Helen behind us may be a tortoise on the course,' retorted Christine spiritedly, 'but all I can say is that the woman's no slowcoach off it.'

Helen Ewell was one of the unspoken reasons why Christine had joined the Golf Club: her husband, David, she knew only too well would be easy prey for a woman of Helen's sort.

'I suggested to Dallas Southon that she joined the Club when we did,' she remarked with apparent inconsequence, 'but she said she'd rather stick to collecting antiques than traipse round the course after Brian.'

'Well, she has got a really lovely collection of old silver,' said Christine.

'Some of her pieces are beautiful and if that's what interests her...'

'I daresay,' agreed Anna. 'But antique silver comes expensive.' She looked back over her shoulder. 'Come along. We mustn't forget the tortoise reached the end first because the hare got overconfident.'

'And Helen can be fast enough when it suits her, I can tell you,' said Christine ambiguously.

'Colin,' Anna quoted her husband again, 'says you can never tell who's won in golf...'

Christine giggled. 'Not until the fat lady sings, eh?' she suggested.

'No. Not until the nineteenth closes,' said Anna.

'You wait,' promised Christine. 'One day we'll beat Colin and David, too. And before the nineteenth.' Her knowledge of the sociabilities customary after the game was still a little limited, too.

'Mmm,' murmured Anna thoughtfully. Beating her husband was not on her agenda.

'I can tell you one thing, though,' said Christine, she, too, looking over her shoulder, 'and that's that pair behind us aren't even going to get as far as the nineteenth. Not today, and not at their rate, anyway.'

'Why not...' Anna turned too. 'Oh, I see. One of them's gone and got herself into the Hell's Bells bunker. Oh, what bad luck!'

'I wonder whose ball it is,' said Christine, watching with interest to see whether it was to be Helen or Ursula who set off for the deep bunker behind the green.

'Whose ever it is, I bet she won't get out of there first go,' said Anna, who had had to listen time and again to detailed accounts of his games from her Colin and who thus knew the course better than Christine – in theory, that is. The depth of the bunker behind the sixth green was a hardy perennial when she was being properly sympathetic in the matter of torn-up cards and lost matches.

'It's Helen Ewell's,' said Christine, shading her eyes and staring back at the sixth green.

'Tough,' said Anna, without any noticeable sound of regret. 'You do realise, Christine, don't you,' she added mischievously, 'that there's not a single man in sight to come to her aid?'

'Not even the greenkeeper, poor thing,' said Christine. It was not clear whether it was the greenkeeper or Helen for whom she was expressing her sympathy.

'Oh, the greenkeeper's out of action, anyway,' said Anna. 'I heard he's been off sick all week, which is why the fairway grass is a bit long just now.'

Christine craned her neck. 'I can't even see her now she's in the bunker.'

'So she'll have to manage on her own, won't she?' grinned Anna. 'Ursula Millward isn't supposed to advise her.' She noted with approval that Ursula had taken up a perfectly correct position by the flag, which she was now raising well above her head so that her friend in the bunker might have some idea of the general direction in which she should be aiming her shot.

'Come on, Anna,' Christine urged her friend from the safety of the seventh hole. 'Now we've got a head start we might as well keep it. After all, Helen might give up and just mark Ursula's card from now on. That'd make them a lot quicker and that could be a nuisance to us.'

'Right you are,' said Anna amiably. 'Anyway, we'll hear all about it with a vengeance when we get in.'

'You bet we will. Our Helen likes an audience.'

'Helen likes a male audience,' Anna corrected her. 'I don't think we mere lady members'll do instead when she tells us about her terrible luck today.'

She was wrong.

Anyone and everyone would have done for audience when Helen Ewell eventually got back to the Clubhouse of the Berebury Golf Club. The trouble was that by then her voice had been reduced to a totally incoherent babble that no one could understand.

Chapter Two

Police Superintendent Leeyes checked his watch and not for the first time. He was standing impatiently at the long window of the Clubhouse that looked out on both the eighteenth hole and the first tee of the golf course. Catching sight of some movement near the latter, he turned to the man at his side and said 'Great, they've opened the first tee to us at last. Come along, Garwood. It's gone half-past already and those dratted women should be well out of the way by now.'

'They'll be slow,' Douglas Garwood, a short spry man, warned him. 'Very slow.'

'Women usually are,' grunted Leeyes.

'Rabbits always are,' said Garwood.

'They aren't the only ones,' said Leeyes. He pointed at someone walking outside the window. 'Look at old Bligh over there. He gets slower and slower.'

'It's his knee,' said Garwood.

'Hrrmph,' said Leeyes, resuming his study of the course.

'Old Bligh may be slow,' observed Garwood, 'but he still hits a good drive.'

'True,' admitted Leeyes grudgingly.

'And anyway it's the third shot that counts as time goes by,' said Garwood, 'not your drive.'

Leeyes changed tack. 'And Hopland isn't quick either.' He jerked a thumb in the man's direction. 'Look at the pair of them shuffling into the locker rooms.'

'James doesn't have to be quick,' pointed out Garwood. 'He's as good as retired.'

'I suppose he doesn't play all that badly,' conceded Leeyes.

'For an old man,' rejoined Garwood neatly. 'And there's Luke Trumper over there with Nigel Halesworth waiting to play.'

'I do believe that they're going to go out now, too,' said

Leeyes, irritated. 'We'll have to look sharp to get in ahead of them.' He scowled. 'What's Trumper doing up here today anyway? He's not usually around midweek.'

'Ready when you are,' said Garwood, leaving Leeyes' question unanswered and suppressing any thought he might have had about it being possible to take the policeman out of the police station but not the police station out of the policeman.

'Come along then,' urged Leeyes. 'We don't want to have to play behind a pair of old dodderers let alone Trumper and Halesworth.'

'Patience is good for the soul,' said Garwood philosophically. 'And the blood pressure.'

Leeyes shot the man a questioning look, decided he wasn't trying to be funny, and so stayed silent. This was because the Superintendent, ever afraid of being seen in the wrong company, was always careful with whom he played. He never had any qualms in arranging a game with Douglas Garwood. Circumspection was not necessary with the man. Calleshire Consolidated, Plc., of which Company Doug Garwood was the chairman, had an impeccable reputation throughout the county for honest dealing.

And for making money.

A lot of money.

'Unless, that is,' continued Garwood politely, 'you're in a hurry to get back on duty.'

'No, no,' protested Leeyes at once. 'Not at all. My time's my own today.' The Superintendent was up for the Men's Committee – an important and necessary step on the way to the Captaincy – and was belatedly realising that election candidates had to mind their manners. He gave a deprecating little laugh. 'One of the few advantages of being in the Force, you know, is the occasional daytime off-duty. Not that we don't work when other men play, of course,' he finished piously.

The two golfers left the Clubhouse, collected their clubs and strolled towards the first tee, passing as they did so the old Nissen hut that did duty as the caddies' shed. Leeyes jerked his head in its direction. 'Do you need one of those?'

'Not today, thank you,' said Garwood. He paused and said: 'I do like to have a caddy in a competition, though. It's all very well for you, Leeyes, but I'm not as young as I was, and a caddy does help on the hills.'

'Golf isn't like boxing,' said Leeyes profoundly. 'In boxing a good young one usually beats a good old one.'

'I'm sure...'

'In golf,' expounded the Police Superintendent , 'a good old one beats a good young 'un. Not the other way round.' He sniffed. 'No use getting old if you don't get cunning.'

Douglas Garwood was still following his own train of thought. 'But I don't like it when I've got a caddy and my opponent hasn't, like I did the other day. I think if Peter Gilchrist had had a caddy when we played the third round of the Clarembald Cup last week, I wouldn't have beaten him and got through into the next round. After all, fair's fair.'

'Quite,' said Leeyes insincerely. A working life spent in the police force had left him uncommitted to the concept of fairness. 'It's just as bad,' he added even more mendaciously, 'when it's the opposite way round and the other fellow has a caddy when you haven't.'

'Not really,' said Garwood. 'By the way, Leeyes, where do you stand on the Great Divide?'

The Committee of the Berebury Golf Club was presently trying to decide whether to build a driving range on site to attract more players, selling some land for development in the process to fund it. This had split the membership as nothing else had done since the furore over the admission of the Ladies before the war.

'I'm afraid I have to be neutral,' said Leeyes virtuously,

neatly ducking the issue, 'being a member of the Force and all that. We have to police demonstrations all the time, you know, and nobody's supposed to know what we think. And what about you?'

'It never does to mix business with pleasure,' said Garwood obscurely.

The two golfers continued on their way to the first tee while within the caddies' shed talk turned to the pair coming along behind the two men.

'Who are you going out with today, Dickie?' asked Bert Hedges. He was sitting down on a wooden bench changing into his golf shoes.

'Major Bligh,' answered Dickie Castle, bending down to do up his own laces. 'Second round of the Pletchford Plate.'

Bert Hedges stamped his feet well down in his shoes and nodded. 'He's always in with a fighting chance is the Major – unless he's up against a real tiger, of course.'

'What about you, mate?' Dickie Castle asked him in return.

'Today? A singles,' answered Hedges. He shrugged his shoulders. 'But only a friendly.'

'It's my belief,' declared Dickie solemnly, 'that there's no such animal as a friendly match.'

Edmund Pemberton, a copper-nobbed new arrival as a caddy, said 'A friendly match being a contradiction in terms, you mean?' He was on vacation from the University of Calleshire and had both an enquiring mind and an interest in the meaning of words.

'I don't know what you mean, laddie,' said Bert Hedges heavily, 'but what our Dickie here meant was that friendly matches aren't so interesting.'

Dickie Castle grinned, 'And what Bert means, young Ginger, is that there's usually nothing much riding on a friendly.'

Pemberton, who hated being called either young or Ginger,

had the sense not to take his interest in semantics any further, and changed the subject 'Is this Major Bligh going to win the Pletchford Plate then?'

Dickie Castle sucked his lips and said judiciously 'Whether he wins the Pletchford or not really hangs on who he meets in the round after this one with James Hopland.'

'For his sins,' said Bert Hedges, who hadn't been inside a church since he got married, 'it'll be either Peter Gilchrist or Brian Southon on account of Brian Southon having had a walkover from Eric Simmonds.'

'Eric Simmonds still ill, is he?' asked Hedges.

'I can tell you that it's Gilchrist who won,' another man informed them. 'I saw it on the board this morning, although how he's got time to play I don't know. They say he's laying people off at his works as fast as he can.'

'Those two played their match the other day,' said a man called Shipley. 'Matt went out with them just before he took off and so did old Bellows over there.' He jerked his thumb in the direction of an elderly caddy sitting slightly apart from the others, head well down, and patently deaf to their chat.

Castle nodded. 'I'm not surprised that it's Gilchrist who won. He's the better man, really. Plays a very steady game when he's got his back to the wall.'

'It was close, though,' said the other man. 'I heard they went to the twentieth.'

'The twentieth?' piped up Edmund Pemberton again. 'I thought there were only eighteen holes on the course.'

'When the match is all square at the eighteenth,' Bert Hedges informed him in a lordly way, 'you start again at the first hole though then you call it the nineteenth…'

'But I thought the nineteenth was the bar in the Clubhouse,' said Pemberton naively. 'That's what Matt told me…'

'It's that, too, boy,' grinned Dickie. 'Especially on Sunday mornings.'

'And if you don't happen to win the nineteenth,' persisted Bert Hedges, 'you go to the twentieth and go on playing until one of the players wins…'

'And for your information,' added Dickie Castle chillingly, 'it's called "sudden death".'

'Can you see where the pin is from where you are?' Ursula Millward had called out after Helen Ewell had descended into the steepest bunker on the course. 'I'm holding it up high to give you a bearing…'

'That's not the problem,' Helen called back. 'I've got a really horrible lie, though. I'll have to take my eight iron at least…' This was followed by the thudding sound of club hitting sand, succeeded by a muffled imprecation from the bunker. 'No, this needs a lob wedge.'

Ursula Millward waited.

The thudding sound came again.

And again.

And again.

'The trouble,' shouted up Helen, 'is that the sand in here is so very soft. The ball keeps on rolling back down again after I've hit it and the place it comes back to gets deeper each time.'

'I think the rules say you've got to keep counting,' called back Ursula uneasily. She thought about saying something, too, about rabbits being good at burrowing but suppressed the words just in case the remark upset Helen even more.

There was another thud.

'I am going to get this ball out of this bunker,' said a very determined voice from below, 'if I have to stay here all night to do it.' This was followed by three more thuds in quick succession.

'Take your time,' called out Ursula, even though she could see that two men on the course who had been a long way behind them were rapidly gaining on them – and her own arm was getting quite tired from holding up the flag.

The next thud was followed by a long silence – but not by the expected arrival on the green of Helen's ball.

Curious, Ursula walked across to the edge of the green and peered down. Helen was down on her knees in the bunker, bending over her ball. Then she picked the ball up, tossed it to one side, and started to scrape away at the sand with uncharacteristic urgency.

'Helen,' began Ursula, 'I don't think that's allowed…'

She was stopped by a high-pitched shriek.

'What is it?' she called down.

'Come down here, Ursula,' sobbed Helen in a strangely strangled voice. 'Quickly… there's something horrible.'

Ursula laid down the flag-pin and scrambled down to her side, the game forgotten. 'What is it?'

'A body,' Helen said in a choked voice. 'A head anyway,' she quavered.

Before breaking down completely and lapsing into total incoherence, she managed to stutter 'And I think I've just knocked its eye out.'

Chapter Three
Unplayable

'Switchboard here, Inspector Sloan,' said the voice at the other end of his telephone. 'Message for you from the Superintendent.'

'But he's not in today, surely, Melanie?' said Detective Inspector CD Sloan, puzzled. He was certain of that. It was one of things that all those at Berebury Police Station always knew instinctively without being told.

'No, sir,' agreed the voice on the switchboard. 'He isn't in.'

'So?' When Superintendent Leeyes was in the building it had the same effect on his underlings as did the arrival of a sparrowhawk on a garden full of little birds. Everyone there then lay very low and quite still, heads well down. When the Superintendent wasn't there everyone went about their usual avocations no less dutifully but in a more relaxed manner.

'He says he wants you urgently.'

'So how come he wants me urgently, then, if he's off-duty today?' Detective Inspector Sloan was Head of the tiny Criminal Investigation Department of "F" Division of the Calleshire County Constabulary at Berebury. Known as Christopher Dennis to his friends and family, the Inspector was for obvious reasons called "Seedy" by his colleagues at the Berebury Police Station.

'He was ringing from the Golf Club,' explained the telephonist.

He should have guessed. Superintendent Leeyes might possess a perfectly good house in a pleasant part of the old market town and work at the Police Station in the not-so-nice High Street, but to all intents and purposes he lived and had his being on the golf course. 'But why?'

'All I know is that he wants you and your team over there at the Club quicker than soonest,' said Melanie, lapsing into the vernacular. 'Like pretty smartish.'

'All right, then.' Detective Inspector Sloan grinned to himself. There was only one other person who would be glad to know that Sloan was on his way to the Golf Club and that was his own wife, Margaret. 'You can tell him I'm on my way.'

In spite of his protests to the contrary, Margaret Sloan was quite convinced that therein – membership of the Golf Club – lay the only way to promotion. He'd lost count of the number of times that he'd told her that he didn't see how hitting a small white ball for the number of times it took to walk three and a half miles up hill and down dale in pursuit of that same small white ball led to an instant rise in rank. And that he preferred growing roses anyway.

'As for my team, Melanie,' he went on, quickly suppressing the spectre of having to play against the Superintendent as part of his wife's game-plan, 'you can say that Constable Crosby's the only one around just now...' he stopped and changed this. 'No, on second thoughts don't tell him that.' Detective Constable Crosby was not the brightest penny in the purse: usually he only had to open his mouth to put his foot in it.

'Better to let the bad news wait,' Sloan murmured to himself as he put the telephone down.

'Perhaps, sir,' suggested that very same Detective Constable Crosby, at the wheel as the police car slipped out of the station yard at Berebury and into the traffic stream, 'the Super's lost his ball and needs the detective branch to find it for him...'

'You just concentrate on getting us to the Golf Club in one piece, Crosby.' Sloan put his thumbs firmly inside his seat belt to stop his hands rising protectively in front of his face as the police car cornered at speed. 'And keep the jokes for later.'

'Yes, sir. Sorry, sir.'

'Besides, speculation ahead of the facts will get us

nowhere.' In police work, it could be very dangerous, too; especially – an ever-present worry – when it led to preconceived ideas shutting out other – better – lines of enquiry. But this was something Crosby would have to learn for himself. There was only so much about detection that could be taught. The rest had to be caught. 'Apart from anything else, Crosby, it's a waste of time.'

Superintendent Leeyes was waiting for them on the steps of the Clubhouse. Crosby steered the car as near to him as he could and came to a stop with a noisy flourish of brakes.

'Not there, man,' spluttered Leeyes at the Constable, as Sloan clambered out from the passenger seat beside him. 'Can't you read? That notice says that the parking here is reserved for the Men's Captain. Get that car out of the way before anyone sees you.'

Crosby reversed at an equally fast speed and disappeared in the direction of the professional's shop in a cloud of dust.

'You, Sloan,' commanded Leeyes, 'come with me.'

'Yes, sir.' It occurred to the detective inspector that he hadn't often seen the Superintendent out of uniform, although the police chief wasn't now so much dressed in mufti as appropriately clad for the game of golf, which wasn't the same thing at all.

'This way, man,' Leeyes turned on his heel, and set off at a dog-trot round the side of the Clubhouse. 'We'll make for that practice tee over by those trees. Can't go in the Clubhouse in these shoes. Not allowed.'

Sloan's gaze travelled downwards and took in the fact that his superior officer was wearing brogues worthy of a Highland Chieftain of yesteryear.

'It's the spikes,' explained Leeyes. 'They damage the carpet. Besides, we need to get away from all the Rabbits in there.'

'Rabbits, sir?' echoed Sloan cautiously. If quite ordinary people could lose their marbles, then presumably so could senior policemen.

'Beginners, Sloan, absolute beginners,' he said with a grimace, 'and in this case, which is worse, women beginners. And those in there are making the very devil of a noise.' He snorted. 'No one can get near enough to the ladies to quieten them down, let alone get a decent story out of anyone, more's the pity. Fortunately I was almost first on the scene myself – after the woman who found the body, that is.'

'That'll be a great help, sir,' said Sloan, unconvinced of any such thing. 'So if I might just make a note…'

'You won't get any sense out Helen Ewell and Ursula Millward – that's the pair who were playing,' snorted Leeyes. 'Nobody can. For a start they're all holed up with the other women in the Ladies Section.'

'Ah.' As always, Sloan was glad to get hold of names. Any names. At this stage, at least, it would be something to go on.

'Helen Ewell won't stop crying,' Leeyes blew out his cheeks, 'and none of the women in there with her will leave her to come out and talk to us.'

'What about?' ventured Sloan, resolving to send at once for Police Sergeant Polly Perkins. She had a way, born of long practice, with wailing women.

'The bunker at the sixth, of course.' said Leeyes, unabashed. 'Didn't I say? Now, come along this way, Sloan. We can talk over there on the practice tee without anyone overhearing us.'

The Superintendent had started off leading the way at a good pace but he came to a sudden halt in front of the Clubhouse when he caught sight of a man standing at the foot of the flagpole there. The man was gesturing uncertainly in the direction of the two policemen.

'Don't do anything until I say, Arthur,' the Superintendent called out to him. 'We don't know yet whether the deceased was a member or not. You'll just have to wait and see.'

The golfer thus addressed acknowledged this with a wave of his hand and walked back over the lawn to the Clubhouse.

'We always fly the flag at half mast, Sloan,' explained the Superintendent, 'when we lose a member.'

'Quite so, sir,' murmured Sloan, adding tentatively, 'and you think you've – so to say – lost one, do you?'

'Someone, somewhere has lost someone,' pronounced Leeyes. 'Whose body it is, we don't know yet.'

'But one has been found,' persisted Sloan.

'A dead body has been partially unearthed in the bunker at the back of the sixth green,' said Leeyes impressively.

'Might I ask exactly what sort of a dead body, sir?'

In Sloan's experience there were bodies and bodies: old and new, for instance, and young and old, too. And male and female…

'Difficult to say just from the head,' said Leeyes, 'and I'm afraid that's as much as we've got to go on so far.'

Detective Inspector Sloan drew breath 'A severed head?' Now that was something that hadn't often come his way in all his years in the Force.

'No, no,' said Leeyes tetchily. 'The head's only as much of the body as can be seen so far without disturbing the scene.'

'I get you, sir.' An image not unconnected with the grin on the face of the Cheshire Cat in *Alice in Wonderland* rose and then died aborning in Sloan's mind.

'At least the woman had the sense not to dig any further than she had done already.' The Superintendent managed to convey that this restraint in a lady golfer had come as something of a surprise.

'A clear field is always a help, sir.' Actually it was a luxury not often enjoyed by his Department.

Leeyes shot him a suspicious glance. 'You could do a lot of damage to a cranium, Sloan, with a mashie-niblick if you didn't know how to handle it.'

Sloan paused and said thoughtfully, 'And probably even more if you did, sir.' In his time he had seen weapons take many forms: for all he knew a mashie-niblick might well be one to add to the list. Knowing how to use it was something else.

'It's the best club of all for some lies – the really difficult ones,' said Leeyes seriously. 'Remember that, Sloan.'

'I will, sir.' He hurried into further speech before the golfer in the man completely overtook the policeman in the Superintendent. 'I take it that there is good reason to believe we're dealing with a non-accidental death?'

As far as he was aware golf was not a contact sport although he'd heard often enough of men having heart attacks on the course... He'd always supposed it was the frustration that did it. Perhaps this was something he should mention to his wife...

Leeyes sniffed. 'All I can tell you, Sloan, at this stage is that we're dealing with a non-accidental burial, which is usually the same thing.'

'And in a bunker, sir, I think you said?' Sloan had an idea that the Americans called those hazards "sand traps". He opened his notebook.   ·

'The one behind the sixth green and of course it's unlikely to be natural causes,' said Leeyes, irritably. 'Not out there.'

'Nor suicide unless someone else has buried him.' Detective Inspector Sloan started to spell out in his mind the NASH classification of the causes of death: Natural Causes, Accident, Suicide...

'Which just leaves homicide,' grunted Leeyes. He jerked his shoulder in the direction of the first tee where a little clump of men could be seen to have congregated. 'Naturally I told them to close the course at once. Not popular, mind you,' he said, bracing his shoulders as one who had only performed his painful duty. 'But it had to be done. The Club Secretary agreed with me, of course, and put up a notice straightaway.'

Sloan nodded appreciatively. At the Police Station the Superintendent's actions – however bizarre – did not require endorsement by anyone. It was obviously a different matter here at the Berebury Golf Club. He scribbled some names in his notebook. 'I'll alert Dr Dabbe, sir, and the photographers and the rest of the Scenes of Crime people...'

Leeyes wasn't listening. He was looking back towards the Clubhouse. 'Ah, there's the Captain arriving now. I must have a word with him at once...you go on ahead, Sloan. And take Constable Crosby with you before the fool says the wrong thing.' He screwed his eyebrows into a ferocious frown. 'It wouldn't do for that to happen, you know. Not here at the Club.' He gave a little cough. 'I'm up for the Committee, you know.'

'Walk?' echoed Crosby, the dismay in his expression almost comical.

'Walk,' repeated Sloan. 'That is, Crosby, as in putting one foot in front of the other.'

'But...'

'Repeating as necessary,' said Sloan. That had been the instruction on the last prescription he had had from his doctor and the phrase had stuck in his mind. 'If you remember, that is what men on the beat used to do all the time.'

'Only the PC Plods,' protested the Constable, whose own ambition it was to be transferred to Traffic Division as soon as possible.

'And incidentally,' swept on Sloan, since this was a sore point at the Police Station, 'what the Great British Public would like us to be doing a lot more of.'

'It's all very well for the Numpties,' muttered Crosby, half under his breath. His own wish to be transferred to Traffic Division was only exceeded by the determination of Traffic Division not to have him join them.

'But the public forget that walking the beat doesn't get the villains caught,' said Sloan absently, his mind now on an unknown body, buried up to the head.

National policing policy had never interested Crosby half as much as his own welfare. He looked round. 'Don't they have those little electric buggies here to take you round the course?' he asked. 'I'm sure I've seen old men riding on them – like Presidents.'

'Very possibly,' said Sloan briskly, 'although I must say I haven't seen any

about so far. Come along now.' He looked at his watch and started to time how long it took them to walk to the sixth green. It might be something that it would be useful to know: it was too early to say. There was a little huddle of men standing to one side of the large green as the policemen approached. 'Douglas Garwood,' one of the waiting golfers announced himself to them. 'Leeyes asked me to stay here until you came. We were following the last of the Ladies in the Competition and Luke Trumper and Nigel Halesworth here were behind us. We've sent their caddies back.'

Nigel Halesworth, a tall cadaverous man, pointed in the direction of the green and said gruffly 'It's in the deep bunker at the back.'

'She must have left her club – it's still there, lying in the sand,' said Garwood. 'Leeyes said not to touch anything and we haven't.'

'I don't blame her for forgetting her club,' put in Luke Trumper, a compact figure who looked as if he could hit a ball a long way. 'Done it myself sometimes and that's without finding a body.'

'Pity about all this,' said Garwood, waving a hand. 'Enough to put the woman off her game forever.'

'Golf's a difficult enough game as it is,' chimed in Halesworth. 'You have to concentrate so.'

Detective Inspector Sloan decided that this was something he must remember to tell his wife, too, although his own immediate priorities were different. He moved cautiously across the green until he reached a point above the bunker. It was indeed deep and steep-sided. Most of the surface was neatly raked but at one point, alongside a discarded club, there were footmarks in the sand. In front of these there was a little space clear of sand in which could clearly be seen the remnants of a human face.

But it was a solitary white golf ball resting a few inches away from that facewhich really added the Grand Guignol touch.

Sloan stood stock still on the green and set about committing the scene to memory, absorbing what he could of the spot's surroundings before allowing his gaze to home in on the battered face protruding from the sand. His silent absorption, though, was not allowed to last long.

Detective Constable Crosby looked up and announced that the picture boys were on their way. 'I bet it's the longest they've had to walk in years,' he said with a certain satisfaction as Williams and Dyson, the two police photographers, approached the sixth green on foot.

'We'd have loaded our stuff onto a golf buggy if we could've found one,' said Williams, panting up onto the high green.

'Apparently they don't have them here,' chimed in Dyson. 'Too hilly.'

'You can say that again,' Crosby endorsed this.

'So they have caddies instead,' said Dyson. 'The lucky ones, that is. Not us.'

'Those cameras must weigh a bit,' agreed Sloan moderately. The man was as hung about as an old-fashioned pedlar.

'Can't do without 'em, though, can you?' challenged Williams.

'No.' Detective Inspector Sloan, veteran of many a court case, would have been the first to admit that photographs, suitably authenticated, weighed heavily in evidence – too heavily, sometimes – with juries. The camera might be able to lie –could and did lie – but it couldn't look unreliable or sound shifty like some accused and a great many witnesses could.

'There's nothing to beat a good old-fashioned photograph for your album,' declared Dyson, plonking his own equipment down on the green with scant regard for the precious Cumberland turf, 'taken with a good old-fashioned camera. It doesn't lie as easily as a digital one.'

'Now,' said Sloan, immediately getting down to business, 'if you'd take some shots from up here first…'

'That ball's in a pretty difficult lie, isn't it?' Williams interrupted him. He, too, had been peering over the edge of the bunker. 'Especially for a beginner.'

'So you play golf, too, do you?' divined Sloan swiftly.

'Too right, I do, Inspector,' grinned Williams. 'I play, but not at your precious Royal and Ancient Club here at Berebury.'

The detective inspector waved at the bunker. 'I daresay we could do with a golfer on the team, things being what they are here.'

'But you've got the Superintendent, Inspector, haven't you?' said Williams, tongue well in cheek. 'He's a member here, surely.'

'Not the same thing at all,' replied Sloan sedately. Somehow he didn't think the fact the Superintendent played was going to be a great help. On the contrary, probably. 'Even though he was first on the scene.'

'After the wailing woman,' put in Crosby.

'And where do you play?' Sloan asked the photographer. He was clearly going to have to get to know something of the game himself. This would please his wife, if no one else.

'Over at the Links at Kinnisport, thank goodness.' Williams started to set up his camera.

'Isn't that the same thing as a course?'

Williams shook his head. 'Not quite. Links is a Scottish name for sand which has ceased drifting and become more or less solidly covered with turf.'

'Hoots, mon,' muttered Crosby.

'And good for golf, I take it?' said Sloan, ignoring this.

'I'll say,' said Williams. 'Besides they aren't so toffee-nosed over there as they are here at Berebury. We play against this lot in matches and that sort of thing, of course, but we get the feeling that they look down on mere tradesmen such as the likes of us.'

'Craftsmen, if you don't mind,' interjected Dyson, setting up a tripod. He smirked. 'Although on a good day I don't mind being called a specialist.'

'Even when you beat them?' enquired Crosby with genuine interest.

'Especially when we beat them,' said Williams cheerfully. 'Now, what exactly do you want pretty pictures of, Inspector?'

'The bunker first,' began Sloan, 'including all the footprints in there.'

'What on earth did she use to hit that ball with?' asked Dyson, leaning over the edge of the green as well and regarding it with the detached interest which went with his calling. 'A shovel?'

'A wedge,' Williams answered him absently. 'Can't you see? It's lying in the bunker over there near the grass. I reckon it's the only club that would get you out of a bunker this deep.'

'Only it didn't, did it?' said Crosby.

'Someone hasn't half made a mess of trying, though,' observed Dyson. 'Churned the sand up good and proper.'

'That's because when you're in a bunker you have to hit about two inches behind the ball to get the lift,' explained his fellow photographer, starting to focus his lens on what was visible of the victim's face protruding through the sand. 'You chop the plugged ball with an open blade and take a lot of sand. It's called a poached egg shot.'

Crosby looked disbelieving, while Sloan realised that like it or not he would now have to take a proper interest the game until the case was cleared up.

If it ever was.

Jack the Ripper had had his way with young women without ever being caught: something never forgotten inside – or outside – police circles.

'And when you don't get it out the first time,' carried on Williams mordantly, 'you have to do it again. And again. And again.' He waved a hand. 'Soon spoils your card, I can tell you.'

'I can well believe it,' said Sloan, thankful that his own hobby was growing roses. What spoiled those were more manageable black spot and greenfly.

The camera shutter clicked again and again. 'Now, what?' asked Williams.

'Some close-ups of the grass beyond, next,' said Sloan. 'And anywhere where there might be extra sand. It must have been put somewhere while a hole was dug for the body.'

'And the body parked somewhere else,' contributed Crosby.

'Will do,' said Williams obligingly.

'If there is a body, that is,' added Crosby.

'And there may still be footprints in the grass.' Detective Inspector Sloan persisted with his requirements in spite of Crosby's unhelpful coda. There had been stranger things than bent and broken blades of vegetation that had come to the aid of an investigation: there had been forensic entomologists and their decay-hungry little beetles whose evidence had clinched a case.

'Consider it done,' said Williams largely. 'And then?'

'The general layout of the green and bunker,' said Sloan. 'Oh, and the pattern of the raked sand in the other bunkers round about here as well as in this one.'

'Good thinking for a non-player,' nodded Williams approvingly. 'Someone must have smoothed this one over afterwards. Mind you,' he added righteously, 'in theory a player is supposed to leave the bunker in as good a condition as he found it.'

'"Please remember, don't forget",' chanted Crosby, '"Never leave the bathroom wet". My landlady's got that hanging up on a card behind the door…'

'What we don't know yet,' said Sloan, leaving aside the educational works of the late Mabel Lucie Attwell, 'is whether whoever disturbed the bunker in the first place is a golfer or not.'

'Or who it was who's in there,' volunteered Crosby helpfully.

'Pix of an unidentified head, then,' said Williams, unpacking something like an archaeologist's measuring stick. 'Make a note of that, Dyson.'

Dyson, who was busy changing a camera lens, nodded.

'And first views of crime scene.' Williams jerked his shoulder. 'How much of the course do you want, Inspector?'

'The approach, for starters.'

'As any good golfer will tell you,' the photographer said neatly, 'it's the approach shot that counts. Never up, never in, of course, too.'

Detective Inspector Sloan didn't need telling. A lot of good policing came down to the right approach. Especially at domestics.

Williams pointed his camera down into the bunker. 'No use asking this one to watch the birdie, though, is it?'

'None,' said Detective Inspector Sloan repressively.

'Nothing to watch it with,' added his detective Constable unnecessarily. 'Not now.'

Woman Police Sergeant Perkins, familiarly known at the Police Station as Pretty Polly, pushed open the door in the Golf Clubhouse marked "Lady Members Only" without ceremony. She was dressed in mufti and looked as if she could have swung a golf club with the best of them. She didn't need to ask for Helen Ewell. An incoherent, tear-stained young woman was very much at the centre of a circle of would-be comforters.

The only woman who looked up as the policewoman came through the door was older and had been standing attentively to one side of the group. She advanced, hand outstretched. 'I don't think I know you. Are you a new member?' she said to Polly Perkins. 'If so, welcome, although I'm afraid you've arrived at a rather awkward moment.'

'Sergeant Perkins,' said Polly. 'Police.' As job descriptions went, she found that was usually enough.

It was quite enough for the Lady Captain. 'Thank goodness you've come,' she said fervently. 'We can't do anything with Helen...'

Sergeant Perkins was unsurprised. Her daily round was fairly evenly divided between those who were very glad indeed to see the police arrive and those who most definitely weren't. As far as she was concerned both groups meant work.

'And whatever we say to her,' said the Lady Captain, 'she won't stop crying.'

'I understood,' began Sergeant Perkins, looking round, 'that there were two women players involved...'

The Lady Captain pointed to another door. 'Poor Ursula Millward is in the cloakroom, being sick. She saw the face, too.' She shuddered. 'Or, rather, what was left of it.'

'But no one else has seen the – er – deceased?'

'No other Lady member,' the Lady Captain assured her. 'I can't tell you about the men.'

Polly Perkins took another look at Helen Ewell. Her comforters, like those of the unfortunate Job, didn't appear to be having much success. 'Did everyone know that the ladies would be playing this morning?' she asked.

'Oh, yes,' said the Lady Captain intelligently, 'but most people only knew that it would be ladies playing, not that it would be the Rabbits' Competition.' She gestured out of the window in the general direction of the course. 'It's for absolute beginners, you know. Very few experienced players risk getting in the bunker behind the sixth. They usually play short to be on the safe side.'

'And how exactly would everyone else know it would be the ladies playing?' Sergeant Perkins contrived to keep a weather eye on the door to the cloakroom, while from time to time watching the face of the young woman still babbling incoherently to her audience.

'There was a notice outside the Clubhouse reserving the first tee for the ladies between certain times.'

'And what if the men had wanted to play then?' enquired Sergeant Perkins with genuine interest. In her usual world of battered wives and victims of rape and child abuse simple notices saving anything from men for women didn't carry overmuch weight.

'They have to start at the tenth tee and play the last nine holes before the first nine,' said the Lady Captain confident that the rule of law applied at the Berebury Golf Course.

'And,' enquired the policewoman, 'does the way to the tenth pass the sixth green?'

'Oh, I see...no, no, it doesn't. Nowhere near. Ah, here's Ursula Millward now.'

Sergeant Perkins took a statement from a pale but resolute Ursula Millward before turning her attention to Helen Ewell. Banishing all her audience save the Lady Captain, she pulled up a chair half beside, half in front of that young woman, announced that she was a police sergeant and waited in silence. This technique, honed on real victims of real injuries, worked in the end.

The only trouble was that it didn't add anything to what the police already knew.

The first tee of the Berebury Golf Club was not the only place where news of the shutting of the course had not been well received. They weren't happy in the caddies' shed either. A course closed to players had unwelcome financial implications for some.

'Had you been going to go out today?' someone asked a tall thin man called Shipley. 'Before they shut everything down to everyone, that is.'

'Shut it down to everyone except Bobby Curd, you mean,' growled Fred Shipley morosely. 'I bet he'll get in as usual.'

Edmund Pemberton, still new to the game, piped up 'Who's Bobby Curd, then, that he gets to go out and we don't?'

'Bobby Curd,' Fred Shipley informed him, 'is the man who deprives you and me of our rightful perks on the course.'

'I wasn't told anything about perks,' murmured Edmund Pemberton. 'I thought I just got the money for caddying.'

'Balls,' said Shipley pithily.

Edmund Pemberton was still of an age to flush and did so as only the young and freckled can. 'Balls?' he echoed uncertainly.

'Golf balls, lost, stolen and strayed,' explained Shipley. 'Mostly strayed, and mostly into the Gulf Stream…'

'But that's in…' began Edmund.

'The Gulf Stream, boy,' said another caddie, taking pity on him, 'is the name of the wee tributary of the River Alm that runs across the fairway at the fifth.'

'Which is not what golfers call it when their balls go in it, I can tell you,' said Shipley. 'You just wait until you hear some of 'em carrying on about it.' He jerked his thumb in the direction of an older man sitting at a distance. 'The only one who doesn't mind what they say is old Belloes over there.'

'Broad-minded?' suggested Pemberton innocently.

'Stone-deaf.' He grinned. 'His real name is Beddoes.'

'So where does this Bobby Curd come in, then?' asked Edmund Pemberton hastily. His capacity for sticking to the point had always stood him in good stead when writing his essays at College.

'Where he comes in is through the bridleway beyond the

sixth,' said Shipley literally.

'And when he comes in,' said another man, 'is during the night.'

'To steal the balls, you mean?' asked Edmund.

'Quick, isn't he?' marvelled Shipley, who considered formal education a waste of time and money.

'For a student,' said the other caddie, straight-faced.

Pemberton searched wildly for a new subject. 'If Major Bligh beats Mr Hopland in this round...'

'If...'

'And then his match against Mr Gilchrist...'

'A bigger "if", that,' said Dickie Castle, pursing his lips. 'Gilchrist's a good player.'

'Got a lot on his mind, though, with things in the trade being what they are,' said Bert Hedges. 'I heard he was laying folk off at his plant.'

'Will the Major then go on to win this Plate thing?' persisted a terrier-like Pemberton.

'Should do, young Edmund,' said one of the men, 'always supposing that Fred's advice to him is better than yours would have been.'

'And always bearing in mind,' said someone else slyly, 'that Fred here plays off four himself.'

'Mine?' squawked Pemberton in alarm. 'I couldn't advise anybody. I thought all I had to do was to carry a man's clubs round. That's what Matt told me.'

'You thought caddying was a doddle, didn't you?' Fred Shipley pointed a bony finger towards Edmund Pemberton's chest. 'Well, let me tell you, young Ginger, that it isn't. Especially when it's a needle match like the Pletchford Plate or the Clarembald Cup.'

Edmund flushed to the roots of his hair again. 'But Matt said there was nothing to it...'

'Ah, but Matt's not here, is he?' said Shipley. 'Matt's off

enjoying his precious gap year in some God-forsaken spot...'

'Lasserta, actually...' said Pemberton, adding pedantically, 'and as it happens they've got gods there, lots of them, actually. And,' he hurried on, catching sight of Shipley's expression, 'it isn't exactly a gap year either – it's part of his degree course at Uni. He's reading business studies and economics and he needs to get more language experience.'

'...That he said he wanted all his caddying money for,' finished Shipley, showing an equal capacity for sticking to the point.

'Gap year!' exclaimed somebody else richly. 'Never had one of them when I left school. It was straight to work for me the next morning, like it or not.'

Edmund Pemberton decided against saying that things were different these days. He'd found that sentiment better left unsaid in his home circle, too. He sought clarification on another front instead. 'What you're saying then is that if someone I'm caddying for loses his match it'll be my fault?'

'It won't be your fault,' said Fred Shipley kindly, 'but you'll get the blame.'

'And,' another man said solemnly, 'if nobody else sees to that Fred here will.'

Edmund looked from one weather-beaten face to another and decided to keep his mouth shut.

'Although,' went Fred Shipley conversationally, 'you might get let off a little on account of your not knowing the game.'

'Or the course,' threw in someone else.

'So how did Matt manage then?' asked Pemberton. 'He isn't a golfer.'

'Quick learner was what he was,' said Shipley. 'Very quick.'

'Talk himself out of any trouble, that lad,' said a caddie at the back of the shed. 'He might not have known anything about the game when he started but he still got to be a good man on the bag pretty smartly.'

Fred Shipley finished tying his shoelaces and straightened up. 'Bit of a clever-clogs, though, all the same.'

'I can't see where that comes into caddying,' said Edmund Pemberton unwisely.

Shipley gave a short laugh. 'You will.'

'Matt bet the farm on that old codger Garwood beating Gilchrist for the Matheson Trophy even though he wasn't carrying for him,' another caddie informed him.

'And did he?' asked Pemberton. 'Beat him, I mean?'

'How else did you think your friend was able to get off on that world trip of his so soon?' asked Shipley.

'But Matt wouldn't bet on a certainty, surely?' said Pemberton seriously.

Several men who would have been very happy to do just that stared at him in silence.

'Betting on a punter's chance is a risky business,' remarked Shipley after a moment.

'Anyway,' said Edmund, who wasn't sure that he understood this, 'I thought you said that Mr Gilchrist was a good player.'

'Oh, he's got the length and the discipline,' said Shipley. 'I grant you that. What he didn't have the day he played the Matheson Trophy was his ball.'

'Lost?' said Edmund.

'Twice,' said Shipley succinctly. 'So Garwood won hands down, didn't he?'

'Funny, that,' said someone else.

'It serves Gilchrist right,' growled Shipley 'for going out without a caddie in a big match. Cheapskate. Taught him a lesson, though, that did. He had one all right in his round of the Kemberland Cup against Luke Trumper.' He poked his finger at Pemberton's chest. 'Your friend Matt caddied for Trumper in that game and there was no funny business about losing two balls then.'

Before Edmund Pemberton could ask what was so funny about losing two balls in a match, the door of the caddies' hut swung open and a female voice shouted 'Are you all decent? Can I come in?'

The question was greeted with total silence as an attractive young woman walked in without waiting for an answer. She was dressed in a short frayed denim skirt with a strappy halter-neck blouse. In between these two garments a toned swathe of her navel and surrounding midriff was clearly visible.

The physical temperature of the hut might have been far from warm before she arrived but as she came into the building the emotional temperature rose almost palpably.

'What are you all staring at?' she demanded. 'You know what a woman looks like. You might as well get used to my face, anyway. You're going to see a lot of it from now on.' She stared round at the silent array of unresponsive male faces. 'There's no law about caddies not being female, you know. If you didn't know, it's called Equal Opportunities.'

'Hello, Hilary,' said Edmund Pemberton weakly.

'Not exactly a lot to go on, is it, Inspector? Half-a-face.' The Consultant Pathologist to the Berebury District General Hospital, Dr Hector Smithson Dabbe, had arrived on the scene with a flourish on the greenkeeper's truck. 'Although I must say I've had less in my time. Much less.'

Detective Inspector Sloan decided this was no moment to say that small was beautiful and waited instead while the pathologist's assistant, a perennially silent man called Burns, unloaded the pathologist's bags.

'Wish we'd found that truck,' said Crosby. 'Riding beats walking any day.'

'At least,' said the pathologist, taking his first look over the edge of the bunker, 'whoever it is in there isn't going to be troubled by the clangour of the butterflies on the green any more.'

'No, doctor.' Sloan was non-committal. Butterflies – noisy or not – were not a problem on his roses.

'And the face isn't frozen, nor even chilled,' observed the pathologist, still looking down into the bunker, 'but ambient.'

'Yes, doctor.'

The golfers who had been standing sentinel were still keeping their distance on the fairway side of the green, as silent and attentive as mourners.

'And I daresay, Sloan,' said the pathologist with mock solemnity, 'you don't want me putting my great big feet anywhere near the deceased until you've examined the surroundings.'

'No,' agreed Sloan smoothly, 'but I do want to know how long that head's been buried in the bunker.'

'And if there's a body attached to it,' put in Crosby from the sidelines.

'That, too, and a good deal more, if I know the constabulary,' murmured the pathologist. 'Burns, my voice-recorder, please...'

'The approximate date of death would be a good start, doctor,' said Sloan. So, too, he thought to himself, would be a name but the subject's identity was not the pathologist's province. This medical man dealt only with dead bodies; a surgical practice that constituted an altogether different ball game from treating live patients. Names were a police matter and someone back at the Police Station would even now, he hoped, be checking their list of persons reported missing. None immediately came to his mind.

'All in good time, Sloan, all in good time.' The pathologist was staring down into the bunker. 'What we could do with here are some archaeologists.'

'It's not an old body,' protested Sloan. He winced. 'You can see that from here.' It wasn't a pretty sight either but that was not for him, a supposedly case-hardened police officer, to say.

'They're the ones who know how to get bodies out of sand intact, though,' said Dr Dabbe. 'Otherwise it's going to be something of a problem.'

'So must have been getting it in,' said Crosby. 'Unless there's just the head there under the sand.'

'Oh, I wouldn't say that,' said the pathologist casually. 'Sand is easy enough to dig out. Beats soil any day for labour-saving. Remember that, Sloan.'

'And in due course,' said Sloan, nodding, 'we're also going to want to know the cause of death.' In his experience, that was one of the quicker ways to narrow a field of suspects: each murderer to his own method, so to speak.

'We won't forget that, Burns, will we?' responded the pathologist jovially.

'No, doctor,' said his assistant dutifully.

'We need to know why a body has been put here, too,' said

Sloan, thinking aloud. He looked round at the deserted golf course. 'Here of all places.'

'If there is a body,' said Crosby.

'He's as bad as Mr Dick, isn't he?' said the pathologist pointing at the Constable.

'Mr Dick?' asked Sloan, his mind on the job. Why the body had been put there was his problem, of course, not the pathologist's. Dr Dabbe, of all people, took bodies as and where he found them.

'"King Charles' head" was always very much on the mind of David Copperfield's friend, Mr Dick,' said Dabbe.

'Really?' said Sloan politely. At least there was nothing mysterious about the way in which King Charles had lost his head, which as far as he was concerned gave it the edge – so far – on the one in the bunker.

The pathologist wasn't listening any more. He was peering as far over the edge of the green as he could without toppling over. 'I can advise you from here, gentlemen, that the injury said to have been inflicted by your lady golfer – what might be called a traumatic enucleation – was performed post mortem, although I daresay you didn't need me to tell you that.'

'No,' agreed Sloan, who really wanted to be told something he didn't know or hadn't guessed. 'So we've got to wait, have we, doctor, for any more definite information about the deceased?'

'Don't rush me, man,' the pathologist, thus challenged, wriggled forward and peered down. 'I think I can see...yes...I can. The supra-orbital ridges, or rather, what's left of 'em, are just visible.'

Detective Inspector Sloan reached for his notebook and waited.

'They're more pronounced in the male than in the female,' said the pathologist.

'So?' said Detective Constable Crosby, in whom his

superiors had so far failed to instil the correct police proto-
col for interaction with their professional colleagues.

'I should say that your body is male,' said Dr Dabbe, in no
way put out by this informality.

Sloan was obscurely relieved to hear this. He'd seen altogether too many bodies of young girls for his liking who had
come to grief in remote spots in the countryside. They'd
often had shallow graves, too.

'Male?' muttered Detective Constable Crosby under his
breath. 'That's a great help, that is. Might as well talk about
fifty-fifty.'

Detective Inspector Sloan decided he hadn't heard that.

'Male,' repeated the pathologist. 'It has to be either *rouge or
noir* on the roulette table, of course, but I agree matters are
not always as clear-cut as once they were, transsexuals being
what they are.'

Detective Inspector Sloan decided that he hadn't heard
that either.

'Or had been,' said Dr Dabbe.

Or that.

It was easier.

Chapter Six
Loss of Stroke and Distance

It being an exceedingly ill wind that blows no one any good, the bar of the Berebury Golf Club was doing a brisk trade. Golfers deprived of a game had only three places to turn. Since two of these were the practice hole and the putting green, the other – the bar – was busy.

'Two halves, please, Molly,' said Brian Southon to the woman behind the bar, 'and have something for yourself.'

Molly, a calm, statuesque woman built on generous lines, acknowledged this with a quick smile of thanks, and busied herself at a beer engine, at the same time as skilfully catching the eye of the next person waiting for her attention.

'What are you doing here on a weekday morning, Brian?' a man nearby asked. 'I thought you worked for a living.'

'Client meeting.' Brian Southon, a short, stocky man, grinned and pointed to his neighbour. 'Got to talk turkey with my friend Gilchrist here.'

'As long as the boss doesn't catch you out and about, that's all.'

'I'm told my revered employer's out on the course just now,' said Southon, quite relaxed. 'And he won't mind because I'm doing really great business for Calleshire Consolidated. That's right, Peter, isn't it?'

'It sure is,' said Peter Gilchrist warmly.

'There you are then,' said Southon, looking round and smiling. 'Everyone's pleased. That's what I like.'

'It's what they will persist in calling a "win-win" situation, I suppose,' said a man called Moffat sourly. He was a retired schoolteacher and English had been his specialist subject.

'Exactly,' said Brian Southon, 'and that's what every salesman likes.'

'Mind you, Brian,' Gilchrist said, 'I shall have to go back to the office and do my sums before I sign anything.'

'Even his card?' called out some wag.

'I might start to worry if he got too many birdies,' admitted Gilchrist, looking wryly at Southon. 'But I don't think he will, somehow. After all, he's not that good a player.'

'Who wouldn't worry about too many birdies?' said Gerald Moffat, who had been made preternaturally suspicious by a lifetime in the teaching profession. 'Especially with the greens as they are just now.'

'What's wrong with the greenkeeper then, that he can't keep up with the grass cutting?' asked someone else. 'It's not as if we've had that much rain.'

'Tummy bug was what his wife said to the Secretary,' he was informed.

'That's a gastrointestinal upset to you, Moffat, I suppose,' joked Southon. 'Got to keep the English standard up, haven't we?'

Moffat muttered something inaudible into his drink.

'At least the greens are all right now,' said Southon, taking a sip of his beer. 'Peter here and I gave Alan Pursglove a hand with cutting some of them a couple of evenings ago, didn't we Peter.'

'We did,' agreed Peter Gilchrist, the plumpish man thus addressed. 'Hard work it was, too, getting them just right.'

'So that no one could say that you let the grass grow under your feet, I suppose,' said Moffat uncharitably.

'Brian certainly doesn't do that,' said the man called Luke Trumper. He put his hand on Southon's shoulder. 'Never let it be said that our Brian doesn't do his bit for the Club.'

'I shouldn't be at all surprised,' went on Moffat sarcastically, 'if he hasn't got a "to-do" list as well. Nobody'll leave the English language alone these days.'

'Hey, it isn't all me, fellows,' protested Southon. 'Someone else on the Greens' Committee was going to tackle the others yesterday evening.'

'United Mellemetics won't like you two doing a deal,' said a man standing beside the Gilchrist and Southon at the bar. He pointed towards a player sitting on a seat in the window.

'Nigel Halesworth never likes anyone doing a deal with anyone else,' said Brian Southon, nevertheless turning and giving Halesworth a long, careful look.

'He's certainly not going to like so much of our business coming your way,' said Gilchrist. 'I hope you've thought that through, Brian.'

'Oh, yes,' said Southon easily.

'United Mellemetics has been one of your suppliers for a long time, Peter, hasn't he?' asked a player who was propping up the far end of the bar. He pushed his glass back over the counter. 'The usual, Molly, please.'

'Man and boy,' said Gilchrist, 'but you could say that Nigel Halesworth and his precious United Mellemetics aren't being as accommodating as Douglas Garwood and Calleshire Consolidated.'

There was a little pause since everyone knew – but nobody mentioned – that Gilchrist's firm was under pressure these days.

'And Halesworth won't like it either,' continued the same man, 'if anything comes between him and the new driving range that his technical people have done the feasibility study for.'

'But they only did the feasibility study,' someone else on the Committee reminded them.

'And the mammal study,' growled Moffat richly. 'Mustn't forget the mammals, must we?'

'Or the archaeologists,' said another voice. 'They've done their geophysical survey, too.'

'It's a wonder they don't want to know about ancient lights,' said Moffat.

'United Mellemetics hasn't got the contract yet, though. Nobody has. It's still out to tender and there's plenty of members' firms who'll want to bid for the work.'

'And for the land,' said a retired banker. 'It's the land that matters, you know. Development value and all that.'

'I still say it should have gone out to open tender,' said someone else. 'Not just restricted to members.'

'I don't see why it shouldn't be kept in-house,' said another man obstinately. 'There's no law against it.'

'Yet,' said the banker.

'And I still say that it's a waste of good ground,' declared Moffat with unnecessary firmness. 'All that a driving range will do is encourage the rabble.'

An uneasy silence descended on the group round the bar. Gerald Moffat was not a man to cross swords with lightly and the question of the driving range was a tricky one at the Club.

'You must be getting a good deal from Doug's outfit, all the same, Peter,' observed the first man after a moment, tactfully reverting to the earlier conversation, 'things being how they are,' he added gnomically.

Brian Southon laughed aloud at this oblique reference to Peter Gilchrist's troubles. 'Believe me, he is. Peter is doing Calleshire Consolidated proud.'

'Just make sure you don't get drawn against Halesworth in the next knockout, that's all,' advised his neighbour. 'Either of you. Or he'll be taking his revenge.'

'That's a risk I'll have to take,' said Gilchrist sombrely.

'Me, too,' said Southon cheerfully. 'But I shan't worry too much. Business is business, you know.'

'True,' said Gilchrist, pushing his glass back across the bar counter. 'Same again, Molly, please. For both of us.'

There was a payphone in the lobby of the Golf Club. Sloan fished in his pocket for some loose change and punched in his own home number.

'That you, Margaret?' he said. 'Chris here. Listen, love, I'm going to be a bit late home.'

He heard a deep sigh.

'Something's come up,' he hurried on. This was absolutely true and what had come up would soon be on its way to the mortuary, which was where he would have to go soon, too.

There was no audible response to this at the other end of the line.

'Work-wise,' he stumbled on.

In the long pause that followed this last Sloan's mind drifted back to when they'd done Shakespeare's play *Coriolanus* at school. Now that was a play for boys if ever there was one: fighting, treachery and war, war, war.

All magnificent masculine stuff, making the schoolroom echo with the imagined sounds of battle, conjured up by heady words. Even so, their teacher had seen fit to draw their attention to the soldier Coriolanus's description of his wife. Sloan had never forgotten it: that great general had called her "my gracious silence".

The class of teenagers had nodded then with what they thought was world-weary sophistication in approval of quiet, undemanding wives. Now, years later, an adult Christopher Dennis Sloan wasn't at all sure that wifely silence was always gracious.

Not this silence, anyway.

He hastened into further speech. 'I'm ringing from the Golf Club,' he said.

That did the trick.

'Where did you say?' asked Margaret Sloan upon the instant.

'I'm at the Golf Club,' he said, adding, with perfect – but not the whole – truth, 'With the Superintendent. Can't say anything more. Not now. Tell you later.'

The finding of the body would be common knowledge in the town by evening.

'Your mother will be pleased,' she said obliquely.

He doubted it. His mother's life revolved round St Ninian's Church in Berebury. She never missed her weekly Bible Study meeting – or failed to expand on it at Sunday lunchtime. At length.

'You won't beat the Super, Chris, will you?' said Margaret Sloan anxiously. 'Not the first time you play.'

'I promise,' he said – and meant it.

'Except,' she added astringently, 'over the head with a club if he makes you late tonight.'

Parthian shots, he should have remembered, had come up in a later lesson.

The girl whom Edmund Pemberton had addressed as Hilary advanced further into the caddies' hut. 'Hullo, Edmund,' she repeated. She looked round at the other men and said 'And hullo everyone else.'

There was a general shuffling of feet but very few answering "hullo's" until Bert Hedges eventually said 'Morning, miss. And what can we do for you?'

'Let me do some caddying,' replied the girl briskly. 'I'm Hilary Trumper, by the way.'

'Can't stop you,' said Dickie Castle, adding meaningfully, 'even if we wanted to.'

'Would you happen to be Mr Trumper's daughter, miss?' asked Bert Hedges.

'What if I am?' she said truculently.

'Nothing, miss. Sorry I spoke, I'm sure,' said Bert Hedges without any noticeable sign of regret.

'How does the system work?' she asked. 'First come, first served?'

'Not quite,' said Castle reluctantly.

'How, then?'

'A regular player books us for a match,' said Castle.

'Or sometimes just for a game,' put in Shipley.

'All right, I'll buy it,' said the girl. 'What's the difference?'

'A match is played for serious...' Dickie began to explain.

'A game is presumably something played purely for pleasure,' interrupted Edmund Pemberton. 'Surely that's the correct definition of a game?'

Everyone present ignored him.

'So therefore a caddy can be booked for either?' concluded Hilary swiftly.

'Or both, surely,' said Edmund Pemberton.

'Oh, don't be such a pedant, Edmund,' said Hilary, turning back to Dickie Castle. 'What happens if a particular caddy hasn't been booked? Do you work on the cab rank principle? Like barristers have to take their dock briefs?'

'She does mean "first come, first served",' explained Edmund unnecessarily.

Hilary shot him a withering glance. 'They know what I mean.'

'Yes, miss,' said Bert Castle hastily. 'The player just knocks on the door and calls out "Caddy wanted".'

'When it's warm we sit outside on the bench in the sun,' said Fred Shipley, who must have caught something of Edmund Pemberton's precision.

'Ships' pilots work on the same principle,' Pemberton informed them gratuitously. 'Taking what comes next.'

'We don't need to know that, Edmund,' said Hilary dismissively. 'What I need to know is how exactly do I get to start caddying here?'

Bert Hedges, visibly fascinated by the girl's bare midriff, began to say something about in her case sitting on the bench and showing her ankles as well as her tummy would probably do the trick but thought better of it and subsided into silence.

'You wait your turn like everyone else, miss,' said someone else.

'You could get a golfer to ask for you,' said Fred Shipley. 'Like your father.'

She scowled. 'Not my father.'

'Or, in your case, miss,' said Dickie Castle, his expression absolutely deadpan and his voice solemn, 'having a word with the professional might help.'

'Do anything to help the ladies, will Jock Selkirk,' chimed in Hedges, winking behind the young woman's back. 'I'm sure he'd put in a good word for you with the men.'

Hilary Trumper gave him a long considering look but said only 'Right, I'll ask him.'

'But no one's going out just now anyway,' said Hedges 'because of this body they've found.'

The girl's head came up with a jerk. 'Body?'

'In the bunker behind the sixth. They're getting it out now.'

Chapter Seven
Provisional Ball

'Teaspoons?' echoed Superintendent Leeyes in patent disbelief. He glared suspiciously at Sloan from under his bushy eyebrows. 'Who says so?'

'The Curator of the Greatorex Museum,' said Sloan. He had returned to the Clubhouse to report their findings at the sixth green.

'You're not having me on by any chance, are you, Sloan?' The Superintendent had commandeered the little office of the Secretary of the Golf Club as his battle station. He was sitting there now amidst a welter of paperwork that had no connection with any police enquiry. Instead the walls were festooned with lists and charts that had everything to do with all eighteen holes of the Berebury Golf Course and nothing whatsoever – as far as he knew, that is – to do with the contents of the deep bunker at the back of the sixth green.

Sloan shook his head. 'Teaspoons, that's what Mr Fixby-Smith at the Museum said were what you needed when you were working in sand.'

The Superintendent's eyebrows came together in a frown. 'Isn't he that funny fellow with the hair?'

'Rather on the long side,' conceded Sloan.

'Wears odd jeans and funny jumpers?'

'That's him.' With an effort Sloan averted his eyes from the Superintendent's clothes. His superior officer was presently attired in a bright green jersey hand-knitted in cable stitch, a pair of elderly plus-twos trousers, and stockings of a yellow and red diamond pattern worthy of a cross-gartered Malvolio. The jeans presumably went with the Curator's territory these days: he wasn't so sure about the Superintendent's outfit.

'Teaspoons!' snorted Leeyes again.

'Mr Fixby-Smith,' persisted Sloan, 'says they're best for

very delicate excavations in sand.' Prompted by the sight of the Superintendent's stockings, his mind wandered away from the matter in hand and back to his schooldays again. There had been trouble getting any boy to take the part of Malvolio in *Twelfth Night* let alone wear yellow stockings. In fact the play hadn't gone down at all well with the English class… He came back to the present. 'And Mr Fixby-Smith says he's done a lot of excavations in the desert.'

The Superintendent rolled his eyes heavenwards. 'Teaspoons…'

'Not spades, he meant,' amplified Sloan. 'And he knows a lot about sand.'

Leeyes grunted.

'It's an adult male in there, the doctor says,' offered Sloan without further explanation. Why males should have brows more ridged than females was something he didn't want to have to go into with the Superintendent now or, come to that, at any other time. Ridged brows or not, the man was never going to see eye to eye with the Equal Opportunities Commission.

'Ah…'

'And dead a matter of days rather than weeks, he says,' hurried on Sloan.

Leeyes pounced. 'How many days?'

'He won't say, sir. Not until he's seen a bit more of the body. But not many. Dr Dabbe insists that any fine-tuning on timing will have to wait until he's done a full post-mortem.'

'And I suppose,' went on Leeyes sarcastically, 'an opinion on the cause of death would be too much to ask?'

'At this stage,' said Sloan diplomatically, 'yes. It's early days yet.'

'Identification?'

'That's going to be difficult from the face,' said Sloan, suppressing any remarks about not even the victim's mother being likely to know him now. 'But Dr Dabbe has high hopes of the teeth.'

Leeyes grunted and changed tack. 'Missing persons?'

'All we can say for sure, sir, is that there's been no one added to our list in the Berebury area for several weeks.'

'A stranger, then...' The Superintendent was strong on the territorial imperative.

'Perhaps.' That wouldn't absolve the police from investigating the death, only make for more work, but Sloan did not say so.

To his surprise Leeyes gave a deep sigh and said solemnly 'I'm very much afraid, Sloan, that whoever put the body there isn't likely to be a stranger. To the neighbourhood, perhaps, but not to the game or the course.'

'Sir?' All information was grist to a detective's mill. What was different was that grist didn't usually come from the Superintendent.

'You'd be out of sight of anyone on the course there,' continued Leeyes reluctantly, 'unless they over-ran the green and actually sent a ball down into the bunker.'

'Which I gather the really good players don't do if they can help it,' said Sloan. The Superintendent was right. It wasn't unreasonable to suppose that whoever had buried the body here had known that, too.

'The hole's a dog-leg, as well,' said the Superintendent even more reluctantly.

Sloan looked up. Whoever had interred the body must have known that, too.

'You've got to play to the left of the big oak tree,' explained Leeyes. 'What you need is a good long drive and then a shorter, ticklish shot with a fairway wood. Too far and you're out of bounds, too short and you can't turn the corner with your next stroke.'

'So you need it to be just right?'

'Just right,' countered the Superintendent, 'and you probably hit the tree. Never up, never in, though.'

There was a lot, decided Sloan, to be said for roses.

'And the green isn't visible from the fairway,' said Leeyes.

'I'll make a note,' promised Sloan.

Leeyes grunted again. 'I'm not dreaming, am I, Sloan? You did say teaspoons, didn't you?'

'Yes, sir.' He coughed. 'Small paintbrushes come in handy, too, the curator said.'

'So, Sloan,' Superintendent Leeyes came back smartly, 'do facts and I'd like some more of them. And fast.'

Misery might make strange bedfellows but in the Ladies Section of the Golf Club it was keeping familiar faces together too. The women remained huddled in a group long after Helen Ewell had been borne away for sympathetic sedation. Held there in the Clubhouse by some common bond too deep for words, and grateful for the continued presence of Sergeant Perkins, none of them wanted to arrive home before their husbands got there.

Instead they clustered round the long windows at the end of the room that gave such good views out onto the course, exhibiting that aspect of flock behaviour associated with safety in numbers. They weren't the only ones with a wish to keep together. Others must be doing so, too, because the putting green in front of the window, normally the place for golfers to pass the odd half hour with club in hand, was deserted.

Indeed, there was little to see from the picture windows until a solitary figure came into view going in the direction of the professional's shop.

'Isn't that the young Trumper girl over there?' said Anna, peering out of the window. 'Luke's daughter.'

'What on earth is she doing here?' asked Christine. 'She's only a child, surely.'

'I didn't know she played,' said someone else.

'She doesn't.'

'I've never seen her up here before.'

'Today of all days,' shivered Anna, who hadn't enjoyed being questioned by Sergeant Perkins about her own round in the Rabbits' Competition.

'She's been seeing rather a lot of one of the students who's caddying here in the vac,' the Lady Captain informed them.

'It's a boy called Matt Steele.' Ursula Millward had declined the offer of sedation herself but wouldn't go home alone either. 'Her people aren't at all keen.'

The Lady Captain shrugged her shoulders. 'But what can you do when they're that age?'

'Very little,' said a mother of another teenager realistically.

'At any age,' groaned another mother, even more experienced in the ways of the young. 'Except keep talking. That's all.'

'Poor little rich girl,' murmured the Lady Captain.

'Poor?' Anna's eyebrows came up. 'You must be joking.'

'Hadn't you heard?' said Ursula Millward, glad to be talking of anything but the body in the bunker. 'Her grandmother's entered the fray.'

'That's all the Trumpers needed,' sighed Anna, 'just when they were trying so hard to play Happy Families for a change.'

'Happy Families!' snorted another lady golfer. 'You could have fooled me.'

'She'll have stirred it up good and proper, if I know old Mrs Trumper,' remarked someone else who clearly did know the woman in question all too well.

'They can't handle the old lady,' snorted Ursula Millward. 'Never could. It's half their trouble.'

'Go on,' Christine urged. 'Tell us what she's gone and done now.'

'Old Mrs Trumper,' said Ursula impressively, conscious

that she had everyone's full attention, 'has given Hilary half her holding in the firm now and promised to leave her the other half when she dies.'

'*Great Expectations*, then,' said Anna, a keen member of the Berebury Literary Circle.

'More like Jarndyce and Jarndyce,' said the Lady Captain, who knew her Charles Dickens – and her Trumpers – better than most.

'So where does the poor little rich girl bit come in then?' asked a newish member curiously.

'There's Tim Trumper.'

'Who he?' asked another member, younger than most, who liked to be thought of being with it, speech-wise.

'Her cousin.'

'So?'

'Childhood sweethearts until a little chick from Calleford with attitude came along and got her claws into him.'

'Now that must have really upset the Trumper applecart,' agreed Christine appreciatively.

'Believe me, it did,' said Ursula Millward.

'And put Hilary's nose out of joint, too, I daresay,' observed the mother of the teenager, well-versed in youthful angst. 'What a family…'

'For family,' said Ursula Millward, 'you can read firm.'

'Or dynasty,' put in someone else.

'Apparently,' said Ursula, 'this Matt Steele's a bit of a go-getter and if Hilary's got a major holding it's going to be difficult for the family to keep the man out of Trumper and Trumper (Berebury) Ltd., whether they want to or not.'

'Tim Trumper isn't going to like having to share the firm with an outsider,' observed someone else.

'Nor are his father and uncle,' forecast Ursula Millward. 'They're still very active, you know.' She looked round to make sure she still had the attention of her audience before she went on 'I gather they're pretty interested in doing the proposed development here.'

'You mean the new driving range?' asked one of them. 'That's pretty small potatoes for a firm of their size, surely?'

'It's not that bit of work that matters,' said Ursula. 'It's the development value of the land the Club would have to sell to finance it that matters. You see grass,' she explained simply. 'They see houses.'

'So that's why the men are so excited about their driving range,' murmured the Club's dim blonde. 'I wondered.'

'Only half of them,' sighed the Lady Captain who had had to sit through the deliberations of the Men's Committee. 'The other half are excited about having the driving range at all.'

'So why is Granny putting her oar in like that?' persisted Anna. 'Doesn't she like their wives or something?'

'Tim Trumper's chick is an airhead into retail therapy,' explained Ursula, 'and the old lady's afraid the girl'll ruin him.'

'And by extension the firm, I suppose,' said Christine, nodding. 'What do her parents say? Not,' she added realistically, 'that that seems to make much difference these days.'

Ursula Millward said judiciously 'If you ask me it's more a case of "No, my darling daughter" than of "O, my beloved father".'

The ladies nodded as one. This they understood.

'They do say,' said Ursula cautiously, 'that Matt Steele is quite clever.'

The newish member, a little unsure still of the views prevailing at the Ladies Section, said timidly 'It is possible for a man to be too clever, isn't it?'

Nobody in the Ladies Section of the Berebury Golf Club had anything to say to that.

Chapter Eight
Lost Ball

Some facts, decided Sloan, were already beginning to emerge. Literally.

'Careful now,' he warned as one of their Scenes of Crime Officers stepped very near the upper edge of the bunker. 'Fall over there and you'll be destroying evidence.'

Since there was no greater crime in their book than this, the SOCO leapt back from the brink with alacrity. Three other men, gloved and white-suited, were slowly and carefully brushing sand away from the buried head and stowing it away in numbered, labelled bags. Watching them like a hawk was Dr Dabbe, the Consultant Pathologist.

'Decomposition beginning to get under way, Inspector,' he called up to Sloan as more of the body appeared, 'but not very advanced.'

'Which means?' Sloan stepped back involuntarily as a whiff of putrefaction struck his nostrils.

'That we have a reasonably narrow spectrum within which to estimate the time of death,' translated the pathologist.

'A time-frame would be a great help to us at this stage,' said Sloan.

'Mind you, Sloan,' said the pathologist, straight-faced, 'my field doesn't cover everything.'

'Really, doctor?' Since arrogance has always been the most common complaint against the medical profession, Sloan tried not to sound too surprised at this admission.

'And I don't know anything about the similium family either.'

'Neither do I, doctor,' said Sloan honestly, wondering if he should get out his notebook. There were always people unwilling to have their names and addresses taken by the police and this was one he hadn't heard before.

'Sandflies,' said Dr Dabbe.

'Perhaps,' said Sloan lightly, 'we shall have to watch out for sandfly fever then.' He allowed that a sense of humour was one way of not letting gruesome work get to you. Some men drank. Some men took it out on their wives instead: which reminded him to tell Crosby to ring his wife, Margaret, presently, to say that he was still detained at the Golf Club with Superintendent Leeyes. And if she asked why, to say that he was stuck in a bunker.

Reminding himself, too, to ask Woman Police Sergeant Perkins what she did when she got too stressed – that is, if she ever did – Sloan waved a hand in the direction of the two photographers, still at work. 'A few more pix, please, Williams, now that there's more to see.'

'Not that his own mother'll know him from anything you take now,' put in Detective Constable Crosby, regarding the remains of a human face from a safe distance.

'You wait, young Crosby,' said Williams, professionally challenged. 'You haven't seen a good touch-up job superimposed on bone yet.'

Dyson, his assistant, jerked his shoulder in the direction of the emerging body. 'If they could do it with Dr Buck Ruxton's wife then, they'll be able to do it with him in there now.'

Early identification was something else on Detective Inspector Sloan's wish-list. He knew he wouldn't be the only one hoping that there would be a quicker way than this: he was sure that Superintendent Leeyes would be positively counting on it.

'And you, Crosby,' said Sloan firmly, 'can take some samples of the sand from other parts of the course. Try the shallow bunker in front of the green for starters.'

Williams leaned forward. 'Bunker sand, specification SS1, I'll bet. We buy it by the ton over at Kinnisport.'

'Who from?'

'Search me,' said the photographer. 'I'm not on our greens committee, thank you.'

Sloan made another mental note and then turned his attention back to the pathologist. More and more of the body was becoming visible now. 'Anything else you can tell us, doctor?'

'Well, he was too young to need to worry about Saturn,' said Dr Dabbe gnomically.

'The planet?' enquired Crosby, puzzled.

'The bringer of old age,' said Dabbe briskly.

'Over at our golf club at Kinnisport,' said Williams, closing his camera shutter with a click, 'we say it's hard luck if you don't make the back nine holes of life.'

'Judging from his carpi,' said Dr Dabbe, 'this poor chappie here wasn't even middle-aged.'

'Carpi, doctor?' There was a limit to being amused by unknown words.

'Wrists to you,' said Dabbe cheerfully.

Detective Constable Crosby furtively pushed back his sleeves and started to examine his own wrists with a certain wonder for signs of youthfulness.

'And if I was pushed, Sloan,' went on the pathologist, 'I'd say the deceased was in his late teens or early twenties.'

'Too young to die, I'd say,' pronounced Crosby moved by a certain fellow-feeling.

'And I'd say,' said the pathologist, older and more experienced, 'whom the gods love die young.' He crouched down suddenly as more of the dead man's head was revealed by the activities of the men working in the bunker. 'Ah...now we're getting somewhere. I think we may be able to tell you the probable cause of death in a minute, Sloan. Give me a hand here, Burns, will you?'

Detective Inspector Sloan leaned forward alertly. Detective Constable Crosby averted his eyes.

'Yes,' called up Dr Dabbe after a minute or two, 'I would

say you could put his injuries down, Sloan, as being consistent with his having had a heavy blow to the left sinciput.'

'Photograph that, too, will you?' said Sloan to Williams.

'There may be other injuries, too, but he was definitely hit from above and slightly in front,' said the pathologist succinctly. 'Hit hard, too. Can't tell you much about what with yet. Not until I can get the skull on the table and take a really good look at it.' He sat back on his heels and added a careful professional caveat: 'And maybe not even then.'

'But with the proverbial?' asked Detective Constable Crosby, demonstrating that policemen, too, could speak in their own lingo.

'Proverbial?' said Dabbe.

'Blunt instrument,' said Crosby.

'Too soon to say,' said the doctor. 'Could have been anything. Anything at all.' He grinned. 'Did you know, gentlemen, that being hit on the head with a soap-dish did for the Emperor Constans in AD 668?'

Sloan admitted ignorance of this riveting fact.

'You learn something every day,' said Crosby laconically.

Sloan, who wasn't at all sure this was true in Crosby's case, asked if there was any sign yet of what the victim had been wearing. Manners might maketh man but clothes mattered, too, in a murder case because they usually came from somewhere traceable.

One of the white-suited figures sat back on his heels. 'We're just getting to the chest, Inspector. Looks like it could be an ordinary T-shirt. Bit dirty now.'

'No logo?' Proclaiming something was common on T-shirts. Rebellion, usually; immaturity often.

'No, sir.'

'Pity.'

'And jeans,' said one of the other men, brushing away even

more sand.

'There's another thing that doesn't help,' called up the pathologist.

'Yes, doctor?'

'Sand and water are two burial mediums which don't leave signs of disturbance behind them for you people to find and measure with your fancy equipment.'

Sloan decided against saying that he didn't need telling that. It was his habit anyway to let people tell him things he already knew: they often went on to tell him something he didn't. He decided, too, against mentioning concrete over-coats: all they left behind in time was a body-shaped hole. Momentarily diverted, he wondered if a body-shaped hole could be offered in evidence...

'And sand has the merit of finding its own level easily after it's been disturbed, too,' said Dabbe. 'Water's better naturally.'

'There now,' put in Crosby, 'a new lady golfer goes out and does what the hi-tech brigade can't – finds a body in the sand. Well, what do you know?'

Detective Inspector Sloan sighed. Having the body found by an amateur golfer was fine by him: what he didn't like to have to think about was the possibility of its having been placed there by a professional disposer of bodies. That would bring a whole new dimension into play. When it came to the perpetrators of non-accidental fatal injuries the police pre-ferred the amateur to the professional any day.

'No one was actually looking for a body here or anywhere else,' he reminded them all mildly. The list of missing persons at the Police Station had been checked now and there was no young man on it. He didn't know whether this was good or bad. But it was a fact, which was something.

'Inspector...' called out Williams.

'Yes?'

'What are you going to be doing with that ball in the

bunker?' asked Williams, police photographer but a golfer, too. 'It's practically new.'

The police photographer was not the only one taking an interest in a golf ball. At that moment the golf professional was looking at one, too. He tossed it in the air and caught it on the way down as a young woman came in to his shop.

'Can I help you?' he asked, slipping the ball into his pocket.

'I hope so,' said the visitor. 'The name's Trumper, by the way. Hilary Trumper.' She leaned across the shop counter and told him what she wanted.

'But who exactly is it you want me to recommend you to, miss?' said Jock Selkirk to the attractive young woman in front of him, taking in at a practised glance her bare midriff and tight jeans.

'Anyone who wants a caddy,' said Hilary Trumper, 'for starters.'

'Most of the members here already have their favourites,' responded Selkirk. 'That is, caddies who understand their play.'

Hilary screwed up her eyes. 'Is that important?'

'Very,' he said shortly. 'They need men who can tell them whether the course is playing long or short, too.'

'Does that matter?'

'A great deal.' He looked at her curiously. 'Might I ask you if you've ever caddied before, miss?'

'No but I've walked round the course,' she said.

'That's not the same thing, I'm afraid. Are you really experienced?'

'Not exactly, but I'm a quick learner.'

'That wouldn't do at all for some of our members. They like the caddy to know the course, and some of them,' went on Selkirk, warming to his theme, 'expect a little advice, especially when it comes to club selection. Good advice.'

She gave a sudden grin. 'Horses for courses, you mean.'

'In a manner of speaking,' agreed Selkirk seriously. 'It's a case of handing the player the club he's going to need for the next shot. The right one. Before he asks.'

'I didn't realise caddies were supposed to do that as well,' she admitted naïvely.

'That and a good deal more,' said Selkirk.

The girl looked round the pro's shop and pointed. 'Mind you, if they only take out a little bag like that one over there then there won't be all that many clubs to choose from.'

'It's not only knowing the right club for the shot,' protested Selkirk, rolling his eyes at this mention of a special lightweight quiver bag much favoured by elderly lady members. 'Caddies need to know about the rub of the green too, and the length of the holes.'

She pouted. 'There must be someone who would like me to go round with them.'

'Plenty, I'm sure,' smiled the golf professional, eyeing the girl's trim figure appreciatively, 'but that's not the same thing at all.' He looked at her and said in quite a different tone 'Now then, tell me, miss, why exactly do you want to do some caddying?'

'Money,' she said simply.

Part of Jock Selkirk's stock-in-trade as a golf professional was the ability to assess the buying power of his customers and he knew to a penny the cost of clothes. Those that Hilary Trumper was wearing might have been casual but they were good, very good. Her hipster jeans were not any old denim but genuine "serge de Nimes", her casual shirt a masterpiece of understated twin needling.

Besides, he also knew the name Trumper. Trumper and Trumper (Berebury) Ltd were one of the largest family-owned firms still left in Berebury and Luke Trumper himself a regular Sunday morning player. Whatever it was that young Hilary

Trumper was looking for on the golf course, it wasn't money. He asked with apparent off-handedness who it was she had walked round the course with before.

'Matt Steele took me out one day before he went away,' she admitted. 'My father took me round once or twice, too, but that was when I was little.'

Jock Selkirk came to an instant decision. 'I tell you what, miss,' he said, 'I think it would be just as well if I took you round myself first and showed you the ropes before you got started.'

'That,' she said with suspicious docility, 'would be a great help.'

'As soon as the course is opened again, that is,' he said. 'There's been a bit of trouble at the sixth this morning.'

Chapter Nine

Halved

The little bit of trouble at the sixth was getting bigger – or, at least, more visible.

'Definitely a fractured skull,' pronounced Dr Dabbe, straightening up.

'Definitely male,' contributed Crosby helpfully.

'As I say to anyone in Accident and Emergency who'll listen,' said the pathologist, wagging a finger, '"No head injury is too trivial to ignore".'

'Yes, doctor.' It was a lesson that the Station Sergeant at Berebury Police Station was always trying to din into his underlings, too. In its way their cells there were almost an out station of the Accident and Emergency Department of the hospital. Especially on Saturday nights.

'Even they,' added Dr Dabbe sardonically, 'couldn't have missed this one.'

'No, doctor.'

'I can't be sure, Sloan, until I've had a better look but I'm tending towards the injury being from a sharp instrument rather than a blunt one.'

Detective Inspector Sloan made a note and asked the doctor again the question that mattered next in the hierarchy of an enquiry. 'How long dead?'

'Don't rush me, Sloan.'

'No, doctor, of course not.' One of Sloan's early lessons from his first Station Sergeant had been that you caught more bees with honey than with sticks. So he added handsomely, 'There's no hurry.' He didn't know at this stage if this was strictly true but murder, once being done, would always be there, waiting upon justice. And Blind Justice never tired of holding her scales.

'Let me see,' said Dabbe, immediately demonstrating that

the old saw about bees and honey worked, 'where are we now?'

'Thursday,' said Sloan.

The pathologist stroked his chin. 'If you pushed me, I'd say, clinically, seven or eight days. But that's only a guesstimate.'

'Thursday or Wednesday,' said Crosby, counting backwards on his fingers. 'Last week.'

'I can't be quite sure until we know when he was last seen alive, of course,' said the pathologist, hedging his bets.

'Commonsense says he was buried on Sunday night,' pointed out Sloan, 'seeing as Sunday must be the busiest day here and so the risk of someone finding him by accident in daylight the greatest then.'

'But I would say killed somewhere else for sure.' The doctor waved at Burns to start packing his bags. 'Get him up and bring him round to me and I'll see what else I can tell you about your Riddle of the Sands.'

'There are certainly no signs of a struggle hereabouts that we can see,' agreed Sloan, continuing with his own thoughts. 'So far, that is.' He would instigate a wider search as soon as he could.

'There's no blood in the sand,' said the pathologist flatly. 'That clinches it.'

'Then we'll have to look for it on somebody's carpet, won't we?' said Crosby cheerfully.

Detective Inspector Sloan only hoped it wasn't going to be his blood and the carpet that of Superintendent Leeyes.

'Of course I'll help you, Inspector. What exactly is it you want to know?'

Sloan had found Alan Pursglove, the Secretary of the Golf Club, hovering in the Club Room.

'That is, I'll help you if I can,' amended the man, keeping

one eye on the door of his office. 'Your man Leeyes has taken over my room and I can't get in there myself.'

Detective Inspector Sloan took his time to respond to the remark, savouring this instance of *lese-majesty* to the full. It wasn't often he heard his superior officer referred to quite so casually. The good books advised visualising bullies in embarrassing situations as a defence mechanism but hearing the Superintendent cut down to size by one of his peers in this way gave him a perverse pleasure that was much better than thinking of the man half-dressed or henpecked. 'What we need to know first,' he said eventually, 'is when a player was last down in that bunker.'

Pursglove, a short tubby fellow, nodded briskly. 'I can see that would be useful to you.' He shot Sloan an alert glance. 'Let me think how we can work it out. It doesn't happen often, you know. Not there.'

Sloan said dryly 'We think someone might have been counting on just that.'

'So few golfers go out alone these days,' continued the Secretary, 'that I think we can say that this would have been noticed, and so they could be asked.'

'Who else would know someone had been in that bunker?' Confession might be good for the soul but Sloan hadn't yet met a sport where players advertised their failures.

'Molly, the bar lady,' said Pursglove, 'usually hears all the bad luck stories.'

Sloan made a note to seek out Molly.

'And if they were playing in a match or competition,' reasoned Pursglove slowly, 'the odds are they'd have lost the hole.'

Sloan said he could see that they might.

'And if it was a medal round, Inspector, it certainly wouldn't have been forgotten by the player.'

'Medal?' Sloan's knowledge of medals was limited to those

awarded to the police force. In the nature of things few of those came the way of the Criminal Investigation Department, bravery in this area being difficult – if not impossible – to measure. It didn't mean it didn't happen.

'Medal play is when you add up the number of strokes...'

'Strokes?'

'Shots, then,' said Pursglove. 'But it's usually called "Stroke play". It's a question then of getting the lowest total score of all those playing in the same medal competition.'

Detective Inspector Sloan, rose-grower *par excellence*, decided that soon he was going to have to find out the differences between competitions, matches, and medal rounds. But not now. Now he just needed to know how a body had arrived at the sixth hole.

Literally.

'Must have been at night, of course,' said Pursglove immediately when this was put to him. 'And we don't have gates. Anyone could drive in.'

'But not on to the course, surely?'

Pursglove opened his hands. 'Why not? The greenkeeper goes almost everywhere in his truck – he wouldn't have time to walk and get the greens cut.'

'Almost everywhere?

'There are some holes even he can't get to with wheels,' conceded the Secretary, 'which is why we can't use electric buggies here. After all, the course covers a great deal of hilly and uneven ground.'

'But not the sixth?' After all the pathologist had got to the spot quickly enough.

'That's quite accessible,' agreed Pursglove at once.

Sloan nodded. Even now someone should be following his instructions and checking the area for tyre tracks. And the greenkeeper's truck for DNA evidence.

'The course's official yardage amounts to over three and a

half miles, you see,' the Secretary informed him, 'and quite a lot of that is up and down The Bield.'

Detective Inspector Sloan had never measured the area of his rose beds.

'And it's the longest in Calleshire,' said Pursglove with pardonable pride.

Detective Inspector Sloan was quite sure his roses were the best – whatever the opinion of the judges at the Berebury Horticultural Show in a bad year.

'That's not including some spare ground at the south end, Inspector. You'll see it on our map of the course – when I can get into my office I'll show you.' He looked alertly at Sloan. 'We're letting that section go for development...'

'Ah...' Strictly speaking development was a civil matter but in Sloan's book anything that spelt money could spell crime. And development spelt money if anything did.

'Only some of the Committee are still unhappy about it,' ended Pursglove.

Detective Inspector Sloan's head came up quite automatically. 'A Club divided?'

The Club Secretary chose his words with practised care. 'There are those members who want to sell and take the money while the going is good.'

'Jam today rather than jam tomorrow.'

'Exactly.'

'Big money?' Building land must be at a premium out here.

'Very big money,' agreed the Secretary.

'And?'

'And they want to build a thirty-bay driving range with the proceeds,' said Pursglove. 'For starters, that is.'

Sloan nodded. Presumably that would be a money-spinner.

'And upgrade the facilities in the Clubhouse with the extra money. New changing rooms and so forth.'

He could see that that would be a boost to the Club, too.

'Oh, and a new car park.'

'Major works,' agreed Sloan. That car parks were a boon anywhere and everywhere went without saying in some quarters. Including thieves' dens.

'Exactly.' The Secretary said 'So the committee commissioned a feasibility study.'

'Kicked it into touch?'

'Only in a manner of speaking,' said Pursglove. 'United Mellemetics' technical people said there would be no problem.'

'And those against?' At a guess that would be where the problems would be.

The Secretary grimaced. 'They said a lot.'

In Sloan's experience it was always the opponents who said the most.

'They want the money spent on building a decent road round The Bield so that the older members can use buggies.'

'Nobody gets younger,' said Sloan prosaically.

'And a small Dormy House.'

Sloan paused just long enough at this for the Secretary to feel the need for further explanation.

Pursglove said 'Somewhere for golfers to stay overnight. Dormy means that you're in a position in a match where you're as many holes up as there are holes left and therefore you can't be beaten.'

'Bully for them,' said Sloan.

'It literally means that you can't lose even by going to sleep.'

In the police service you could often lose by going to sleep: that was the trouble.

The Secretary went on: 'And there's what you might call a third party view as well.' The man essayed a grin. 'A third party of one. A member called Moffat, Gerald Moffat. He doesn't want either outcome. He says the status quo is good enough for him.'

'A member, man and boy?' They had some dinosaurs on the Police Committee, too.

'Worse than that.' Alan Pursglove looked rueful. 'His grandfather was a founder member and don't we know it!'

'This development...who wants to do it?' Sloan didn't know whether that sort of work could relate to an unknown body in a bunker. It was too soon to say.

'The Committee decided,' said Pursglove, somehow conveying that he didn't agree with his Committee but as Secretary wasn't in a position to say so, 'that the work should be done by the firm of a member. They thought that then it would be bound to be done more sympathetically by people who knew the game and the course well than anyone who didn't...'

Detective Inspector Sloan was sure that a murderer had known the course and the game well, too.

'Without upsetting players and so forth,' said Pursglove.

There was probably no one more upsetting than a murderer, mused Sloan but to himself. Murderers offended against the Queen's Peace – and that was only for starters.

'There's no shortage of firms anxious to tender,' said Pursglove, pursuing a quite different train of thought. 'There's United Mellemetics, Trumper and Trumper, and Gilchrist's lot for a start. I daresay Calleshire Consolidated will want to make a bid for the work, too. They usually do for any work in the area that's going.'

'I see.' Sloan scribbled some names down in his notebook.

'I expect you'll have heard of them, won't you?'

Calleshire born and bred, Detective Inspector Sloan knew them all. Deciding that this was no moment to explain the difference between knowing a firm and it being known to the police, Sloan reverted to the subject of the bunker at the sixth.

'That bunker's not overlooked,' said Pursglove thoughtfully, 'so I would have thought you could dig at leisure.'

Sloan could only dig at leisure. And the garden of his sub-urban semi-detached house was very much overlooked.

'Ideal spot, really,' the Secretary was saying. 'For whoever did the digging, I mean,' he explained. Looking up at Sloan, he said shrewdly 'The professional will have a note of Visitors but you'll be wanting a full list of members, Inspector, won't you?' His face took on a business-like expression as he said in the way of Secretaries world-over when there was trouble in the offing. 'I think I'd better call a Committee meeting.'

'Just a few questions,' said Detective Inspector Sloan comfortably.

'What about?' asked Jock Selkirk. The professional visibly braced himself against his counter.

'Visitors.'

'Visitors?' echoed Jock Selkirk, warily eyeing the two policemen standing in the professional's shop. 'What sort of visitors? Are you talking about players who've bought tickets for their rounds or teams from other Clubs playing against Berebury in matches?'

'Non-members who have paid to play,' said Detective Inspector Sloan, taking in his surroundings of golf bags and clubs and balls and the smell of leather shoes. At the same time he was trying to take the measure of the man in front of him. The professional was not tall but decidedly well-built. He had a good head of wavy black hair, cut short, and the sort of jaw that women called rugged.

'Or who should have paid but have gone out without tickets,' supplemented Detective Constable Crosby to whom the degrees of perfidy had not been spelled out too clearly in training.

'You'll have records,' suggested Sloan persuasively.

'No problem.' Selkirk rummaged about in a drawer behind

the counter and brought out a book of receipts.

'Any of them stand out at all?' asked Sloan, pocketing the book.

The professional started to shake his head and then stopped and gave a short laugh. 'No – wait a minute. There were a couple of guys last month who beat up the course.'

Crosby lifted his head. 'Vandals?'

'No. Scratch.'

'Gave up?' asked the Constable.

Selkirk gave Crosby a hard look. 'I mean really good players who play to the scratch score. It's seventy-one here at Berebury.' He tightened his lips into a wry smile. 'Don't get half enough of those, not men who play to the scratch score. They're mostly Sunday morning types or old fogeys here who haven't ever played to bogey.'

Crosby began to look faintly interested. 'Nothing to do with the march, I suppose?'

'I wouldn't know about that.' The professional gave the Constable an even harder look. 'I'm talking about par,' he said.

'Quite,' said Detective Inspector Sloan pacifically. There were those who needed to have the differences between floribunda, rambling and climbing roses explained to them. 'Anyone else who stood out at all?'

Selkirk frowned. 'There was a south paw.'

'A left-hander?'

'You tend to notice them in my line of business.' The professional waved a hand at a display rack in the corner. 'I have to stock clubs for those on the wild side but I don't reckon in the nature of things to sell that many.'

'No,' agreed Sloan. It was too early for the pathologist to have told him whether the blow to the head of the man in the bunker had been struck by a left-handed man or not. Or, come to that, by a woman. He produced his notebook. 'Any way in which you can tell who was the last player in the bunker at the sixth?'

'Well, I can tell you someone who was in there on Sunday morning,' said Selkirk briskly, 'and that was Brian Southon because he came in here afterwards and wanted advice on shanking...'

Sloan reminded himself that non-rosarians didn't know about rugosa roses either.

The professional said 'He wanted me to look at his grip but I reckon he'd been trying to green it and went too far. Lost the hole, of course.'

'Is it a difficult one?'

Selkirk shrugged. 'Not by my standards. "Tee it high and let it fly" is what I tell 'em. Four hundred and forty-five yards, par four. Bit of a dog-leg but easy enough if you let the wind be your friend. Never up, never in, of course.'

'It's the wind that sorts out the men from the boys, isn't it?' said Sloan. It was the only bit of golfing lore that he knew.

'A fair wind helps,' conceded Selkirk, 'but I always tell beginners it doesn't turn a tyro into a player.'

'Any promising youngsters taken up the game lately?' asked Sloan casually.

'Nobody who's going to win the Open,' responded Selkirk tartly.

Sloan reminded himself that they had their own working shorthand of speech down at the Police Station too. Criminal argot was something that all policemen learned early on, too. "Let's be having you" didn't mean much outside of the world of cops and robbers but it meant plenty to them. He must remember that golfing argot would be something different.

'When did the greenkeeper go off sick?' he asked.

'Joe Briggs? Last Tuesday – no, Wednesday. That's right. They were worried about the greens for the weekend but some of the members on the Greens Committee got together and cut most of them.' The professional gave the police inspector a meaningful look and said 'You're not the only one round here asking questions.'

'I don't suppose I am,' said Sloan equably.

'There's a girl called Trumper, Hilary Trumper, wanting to get to know the course.'

'She's not the only one,' said Detective Inspector Sloan. 'Could you take us round sometime, too?'

Detective Sergeant Polly Perkins might spend much of her time with some very off-beat members of her own sex but she was up to the style of the Ladies Section of the Berebury Golf Club, too.

Well up.

'How kind,' she murmured, metaphorically donning the current youthful equivalent of twin-set and pearls, 'a cup of coffee would be most acceptable. Tell me,' she said, 'this Matthew Steele you are all talking about – is he a player here as well?'

The Lady Captain shook her head. 'Just a caddy. Although,' she added quickly, more aware of the importance of political correctness than most, 'a lot of the caddies play, too. Very well, some of them. Especially Dickie Castle. He beat me hollow in our last Ladies versus Caddies match. He's deadly round the green.' She shivered suddenly, her mouth drooping, 'I shouldn't have said that, should I? Not now.'

The comforting phrase 'I know what you mean, though,' fell automatically from Sergeant Perkins' lips. The things that people felt that they should not have said but did say were meat and drink to the police. And very nearly as useful as those things which they should have said and didn't.

The Lady Captain did not so much change the subject as deflect it. Her skill in this respect was one of the reasons why she was Lady Captain. 'I expect,' she said, 'that Matthew will take the game up in a big way when he gets back. Most of the younger caddies do. It's a very good start to learning the game, caddying.'

'Gets back?' queried the detective sergeant, a woman with an eye for essentials.

'I'm told he's gone off to Lasserta as part of his degree

course.'

'When?' asked Polly Perkins rather more sharply than she had meant to.

The Lady Captain said vaguely 'Some time last week, I think I heard someone say. Is it important?'

In different surroundings Sergeant Perkins might have said sternly, 'The police ask the questions around here' but in the Ladies Clubroom she said 'Oh, no sugar, thank you. Has he gone for long?'

'That's something I don't know,' said the Lady Captain. 'You'll have to ask Ursula Millward over there. She knows the Trumpers better than I do and she might have heard.' She cocked her head to one side and said 'You could try asking Hilary herself, of course. She's sure to know.' The Lady Captain gave an indulgent smile. 'I'm sure they'll be in touch on their mobile phones. Every one seems to be these days.'

'Aren't they just?' agreed Polly Perkins politely, suppressing all mention of the trouble that stealing them had become to the police, let alone of how their use had facilitated the assembling of unlawful protest marches.

'Mobile phones are the second great divide in the Club,' said the Lady Captain wryly. 'After the new development and the driving range, that is.'

'Whether they should be allowed on the course, you mean?' The policewoman, a veteran of many, many hours spent at the Accident and Emergency Department of the Berebury Hospital, where they had to be switched off, nodded understandingly. 'Of course, these days you'll have members with pace-makers still playing.'

'It's not that,' the Lady Captain shook her head. 'It's if your opponent's phone rings while you're driving or putting that so upsets the members.'

Detective Sergeant Perkins said that she could see that it very well might and asked about the proposed driving range.

'Oh, the Ladies are keeping well clear of that one,' said the Lady Captain immediately. 'You know what men are like about that sort of thing. They get very worked up when there's money involved.'

'Don't they just,' agreed Detective Sergeant Polly Perkins, who in her time had witnessed wives who had been beaten up for spending a man's money on food for the man's children.

'I think male pride comes into it, you know,' murmured the Lady Captain, a woman clearly in no need of the odd penny. Detective Sergeant Polly Perkins, a woman still paying off her own mortgage, agreed warmly with her. Policewoman to the core, though, she made a few mental notes before setting down her cup and saucer, and taking her departure.

And seeking out Detective Inspector Sloan.

The Men's Committee of the Berebury Golf Club could have posed for a painting by Rembrandt van Rijn. The players looked as if they were assembled as set of purpose as did the bevy of men in the artist's famous depiction of *The Night Watch* of Amsterdam. A collection of solemn-faced golfers with their game in mind, they took up their positions in the Committee room in silence, taking in the presence of Detective Inspector Sloan and Detective Constable Crosby without comment.

'I think we're all present and correct except for Eric Simmonds,' said the Captain, a former naval officer who'd served his time at sea. 'How is he by the way? Does anyone know?'

'Still as weak as a kitten,' said Brian Southon. 'I dropped in there last night. But getting better slowly.'

'Right.' The Captain clasped a sheet of paper firmly between two large hands.

'Now, you all know about the body at the sixth…'

There were nods all round.

'And that it was not an accident...'

More nods.

'Deplorable, quite deplorable,' said Gerald Moffat automatically. 'We've never had anything like this before in all the history of the Club.'

'Not good,' agreed the Captain gruffly. He shot a glance in Sloan's direction before going on. 'And which is worse, it would seem highly likely that the – er – perpetrator would seem to have been someone who knew the course well.'

'We do have Visitors remember,' pointed out Luke Trumper. 'Lots of them.'

'The police,' said the Captain, 'have details of all the Visitors, guests and Societies.'

'What about Open Meetings?' asked Nigel Halesworth. 'We get dozens of outsiders playing every time.'

'The Secretary has the names and addresses of everyone who has played in our Open Meetings,' rejoined the Captain.

'Players are not the only ones who know the course,' pointed out Brian Southon. 'Don't forget that.'

'I understand the police have taken that factor on board, too,' said the Captain.

'When I was out East,' began Major Bligh, 'we had a feller who went berserk with a kukri...

The Captain overrode this with practised ease. 'Now, Detective Inspector Sloan here will tell you what he wants to know from us all...'

'Ah, there you are, Sloan. Come along in. We've been waiting for you.'

Detective Inspector Sloan suppressed an automatic instinct to wipe his shoes on a mat before he entered the mortuary at the Berebury and District General Hospital. The place was convent-clean, the body of a sand-covered young man the only object not shining and polished.

'Not a lot to tell you yet, of course.' The pathologist waved a hand that already held some arcane instrument whose precise use the detective inspector didn't care to think about.

'Anything would be a help at this stage, doctor,' said Sloan. 'Anything at all but especially a name.'

'Much always wants more,' said the pathologist gnomically.

Sloan stifled an inclination to say that he only wanted information – no, that was wrong – what he really wanted was data. Data was information leading to a conclusion, which wasn't the same thing at all.

'Burns here has everything ready and there's not a lot of clothing to hold us up.'

Pathologist and policeman watched as Detective Constable Crosby and the pathologist's assistant dealt with the young man's clothing, sealing it into separate bags for Forensics, marking each with a number as it began its long journey that would only come to an end in a court of law. That is, thought Sloan to himself, if ever it got to court. Full many a police case was born to bloom unseen and waste its sourness on the desert air.

'T-shirt, underpants, jeans and socks,' enumerated Crosby. 'That's all.'

'Not a lot to be going on with,' said Sloan. 'And from the look of them, all run-of-the-mill clothes.'

'Mass market name tags, anyway,' said Crosby. 'But no shoes.'

'Pity, that,' said Sloan. That arch-observer, Lord Baden-Powell, had set out for all time how much you could tell about a man from his shoes. How, though, you could be sure that wearing out soles and heels equally denoted business capacity and honesty he didn't know. What he did know was that business capacity and honesty didn't always go together...

'No distinguishing marks, either,' contributed the pathologist, 'unless you count a small strawberry-coloured naevus on the nape of the neck. It's very common there.'

'I've got one of those,' announced Detective Constable Crosby unexpectedly. 'A stork beak birthmark.'

'Really?' said Sloan coolly.

'Although all the pictures I've ever seen,' said Crosby, 'have the stork carrying the baby by its nappy. It's pink,' he added.

It wasn't something that Detective Inspector Sloan needed to know at this moment.

'And, judging by the marked lack of sunburn on a strip of his left wrist,' continued Dr Dabbe, 'the deceased had recently been wearing a watch and been in the open air here or abroad quite a lot.'

'You can tell quite a bit from a man's watch,' mused Sloan.

'And a woman's,' chimed in Crosby.

'Such as?' Sloan challenged him.

'That they should be wearing glasses, sir.'

'Right,' said Dr Dabbe, pulling an overhead microphone towards him, 'let's get started.'

Detective Inspector Sloan turned over a new page in his notebook while Detective Constable Crosby drifted away from the body towards the window. He didn't like post-mortems.

'The subject,' began the pathologist, 'is a normally nourished male of approximately twenty years of age. Of quite an athletic build with well-developed muscles.'

'Not a couch potato, then,' put in Crosby from the sidelines. When it came to tackling young criminals he much preferred the couch potato to the well-built. They couldn't run so fast and far.

Or hit back so hard.

'Definitely not,' said Dr Dabbe, continuing with his visual examination. 'Think athletic.'

'I have been,' said Sloan. It was one of the things that being on the golf course did for you. Thinking sunburn was another.

'And, Sloan,' the pathologist waved his instrument like a baton in the policeman's direction, 'you can note that there are no external distinguishing marks other than a surgical scar in the right *iliac fossa*, probably an old appendectomy. I'll confirm that later if the appendix isn't there.'

'Yes, we have no bananas,' sang Crosby, *sotto voce*.

'No marks? Not even a tattoo?' asked Sloan, a little surprised. Tattoos, no longer confined to sailors ashore, were now an important indicator of social significance in the police canon. There was a simple rule of thumb that applied: the more a man had, the lower down the totem pole he was. The same went for studs. Whether the same went for young women he wasn't prepared to say.

'None,' said Dabbe. 'And no evidence of body piercing of either variety.'

'I don't quite…'

'For drugs or studs,' said the pathologist, straightening up. 'No puncture marks from needles and no holes from which gold ornaments might have been suspended.'

'Ah, yes.' Sloan scribbled a note. This was something that it was a help to know: defaulting drug takers, too, had lives that were nasty, brutish and short.

'Just your usual clean-living outdoor boy, then,' observed Crosby mordantly, 'except that he got murdered.'

'Victims come in all shapes and sizes,' said the pathologist.

Victims, in Detective Inspector Sloan's experience, were more often very young girls or harmless old ladies rather than healthy young men, especially the unpierced.

'Nothing of immediate note under the fingernails,' went on the pathologist, 'although Burns has taken samples. And the nails weren't broken – in fact there are no superficial wounds or scratches.'

Sloan put this into police shorthand. 'No signs of a struggle, then.'

'No. At this stage,' continued the pathologist, 'I am prepared to state that the cause of death was consistent with the deceased having sustained a comminuted fracture of the parietal area of the left sinciput, and that this is also consistent with his having sustained a glancing blow from a heavy instrument.'

'Hit on the head,' concluded Sloan succinctly.

'But he's tall,' interrupted Crosby from the other side of the mortuary.

'Which suggests,' said the pathologist, quite unperturbed, 'that the deceased had his head down at the time.'

'I think I get the picture,' said Sloan, thinking golf balls on tees.

'I expect he never knew what hit him,' said Crosby.

'But we want to know what did,' said Sloan. He immediately corrected this. 'We need to know.'

'All in good time,' said the pathologist, reaching for a bone saw.

Detective Constable Crosby took a sudden interest in the view through the frosted glass of the mortuary window whilst the expression "Head first" began to take on a whole new meaning.

Chapter Eleven
Wrong Ball

'Don't just stand there, Sloan,' said Superintendent Leeyes testily. He was still ensconced in the Secretary's office. 'Come in and give me your report.'

'Yes, sir.' Detective Inspector Sloan stood in front of the secretary's desk and began formally 'The body of an unidentified male, age unknown, was removed from a location at the back of...'

'I know where it was,' interrupted Leeyes. 'I saw it, remember?'

'Yes, sir. Of course. Sorry, sir.'

'Well, go on...'

'The victim was almost certainly killed elsewhere and then buried in the bunker at the back of...sorry, sir. You know that.' He hurried on. 'I've got a team doing a fingertip search of the immediate surroundings...

'Ah, Sloan, I was going to talk to you about that... '

'And some other officers are taking a good look at the course generally, especially the wooded bits, to see if we can establish where the deceased met his death. And all the local dentists are being visited with the deceased's dental chart.'

'Good, good.' The Superintendent pushed some of the Secretary's papers out of the way, clearing a space for himself on the man's desk. 'That's what I wanted to know.'

'I would also like to get on with having the locker rooms examined,' persisted Sloan. 'As you yourself said,' he added sedulously, 'the injury could well have been inflicted with a golf club. The doctor says so, too.'

'You do realise, don't you, Sloan, that you're talking about a lot of clubs in there?'

Sloan nodded.

'Valuable, some of them,' said Leeyes. 'And you must

understand some men get very attached to their putters.'

'I'm sure, sir,' said Detective Inspector Sloan untruthfully. It was beyond him to understand how any man could feel affectionate towards a crooked piece of iron at the end of a long handle. One day, perhaps he would. He was sure, though, his wife would like it if he got attached to anything at the Golf Club – but especially the game.

'A man's relationship with his putter is very important,' stated Leeyes profoundly.

'Yes, sir, I'm sure.' All Sloan wanted to know at this moment was whether that relationship had extended to using it to kill the body in the bunker.

'Putting, you know,' Leeyes said, leaning back expansively in the chair, 'is more than just hitting the ball into the hole.' He gave a little smile. 'You might say, Sloan, that is at one and the same time a neurological and a psychological and a mechanical action.'

'I'm sure, sir…'

'Mind you, Sloan, it is also subject to paralysis by analysis.'

'Sir?'

The Superintendent gave a lordly wave. 'You could liken it to writer's block. A four-foot putt can undo a man.'

'That's the most difficult shot, is it, sir?'

Leeyes sat up with a jerk. 'Certainly not, Sloan. They're all difficult.'

'Yes, sir. Coming back to putters…'

'I still play with my father's old hickory-shafted one,' said Leeyes unexpectedly.

'Really, sir?' Suggestions at the Police Station about the Superintendent's parentage had never included anything so mundane as a father with hickory-shafted golf clubs.

'Lovely little head.'

'I'm glad to hear it, sir.' Now that Sloan came to think about it there was a particular pair of secateurs he wouldn't want to be without himself: the parrot-headed ones, honed to the sharpness needed for a clean cut on an old rose. To be fair, he always kept them locked safely in his potting shed.

'Can't be doing with all these fancy things they play about with these days and call putters,' said Leeyes.

Sloan hadn't imagined for one moment that the Superintendent would like anything new – let alone fancy.

'Belly putters, some of 'em are called,' muttered Leeyes. 'Did you ever hear the like of it?'

'Would a putter,' ventured Sloan, 'make a likely weapon?'

'Good Lord, no,' said Leeyes. 'Don't you know anything about the game at all, Sloan?'

'No, sir,' said Sloan truthfully.

'My choice of weapon would be a seven iron,' Leeyes came back immediately.

'I'll remember that, sir.' Not any old iron then, noted Sloan to himself.

'That is,' said the Superintendent unwillingly, 'if the killer is a golfer.'

'He's someone who knows the course,' said Sloan, 'for sure.'

'Not the same thing at all,' said Leeyes robustly. 'Bobby Curd and his pals know the course quite as well as the members and they never play the game.'

Detective Inspector Sloan put another name in his notebook.

'Ball stealer-in-chief,' said Leeyes.

'I don't know that name, sir.' Sloan thought he knew all the petty thieves in Berebury. Only too well, most of them.

The Superintendent leant forward in the secretary's chair and, elbows on the desk, steepled his fingers in front of him. 'Tricky point in law, lost golf balls.'

'Ah.' Sloan did his best to avoid tricky points of law *pour cause*.

'Tricky because the player has already had to abandon the ball in order to get on with the game,' explained Leeyes. 'So technically it's not stolen.'

Sloan nodded. In his book, that just left "strayed". 'Findings, keepings?' he said.

'Courts aren't with you,' said Leeyes mournfully.

That was a feeling that Sloan could go along with any day.

'So Bobby Curd comes in,' said Leeyes, 'and helps himself.'

'After dark?' The distinction between a crime committed in daylight or in the hours of darkness went back to medieval times. Even gas lighting hadn't altered that, let alone electricty.

'Whenever the greenkeeper can't catch him, anyway,' sniffed Leeyes.

'Where does he come in?' The greenkeeper hadn't been there for a week to catch anyone. He mustn't forget that. He made a quick note to arrange for the greenkeeper to be interviewed.

'The water hazard short of the fifth green, usually.'

Sloan reached for his notebook again. This time to make an alteration. Bobby Curd must be interviewed urgently. 'What would that be called, sir?'

'That depends,' said Leeyes.

'Sir?'

'It's a dear little stream if you clear it with your second shot,' said the Superintendent succinctly, 'and it's that bloody drain if you don't.'

'There's something else, sir,' said Sloan.

The Superintendent's head came up like that of a terrier offered a good scent. 'Yes?'

'A member called Moffat bought a new club from the pro's shop yesterday,' Sloan informed him. 'Told Jock Selkirk that he'd lost one.'

'What sort of club?' asked Leeyes.

'A number-nine iron,' said Sloan. The only number nine he

knew had Army medical overtones.

'That's not a rescue club,' said Leeyes thoughtfully.

The only rescue remedies that Sloan knew of were of quite a different order, although he knew there had been a fearsome medieval weapon that had done for all and sundry in battle and that had been called a "Good morning". 'Would a rescue club have done the trick?' he asked.

'Just the job,' said Leeyes briskly. 'Now, Sloan, I've had a word with the Captain and we both think that as soon as your people have finished examining the hole we can go out there and take a look round.' He waved an arm. 'You can use this room as your headquarters now.'

'Thank you, sir.' The words "your people" had not been lost on Sloan. And it was "his headquarters" now, too. With it came the unwritten implication that it would be his blame, too, if anything went wrong in the investigation.

'I just want to show the Captain the lie of the land from the police point of view,' said Superintendent Leeyes. 'Got to keep him in the picture and all that.'

'Sir…' Detective Constable Crosby burst unceremoniously in upon Sloan who was talking to Alan Pursglove in the Secretary's room. 'Sir, they've gone and opened the course again.'

'What!' Sloan got to his feet. 'I don't believe it.'

Crosby pointed out of the window. 'Look. They're all over there. Queuing on the first tee.'

Alan Pursglove coughed. 'Open except for the sixth hole, I may say, Inspector. That's still closed, naturally.'

'I should hope so,' growled Sloan. 'How come?'

Pursglove waved a hand in personal exculpation. 'The Captain asked your Superintendent Leeyes if we might resume play and he said yes.'

Detective Inspector Sloan suppressed his immediate response to this in favour of securing his pension, long term.

'There's no stopping them, is there?' said Crosby admiringly.

The Secretary said 'We consulted the Rules of Golf, of course.'

Sloan was unsurprised. The Superintendent was always ready to throw the Rule Book at anyone when it suited him. 'I take it that that covers every eventuality?' he said with heavy irony.

'In theory,' said the Secretary. He stroked his chain. 'I'm afraid there's a good deal of theory to the game these days, Inspector.'

That was something else for Sloan to tell his wife: that there was much written work to be learnt. It sounded nearly as bad to him as the examination for sergeant and that, he wouldn't need to remind her, had been bad enough. For them both. A young married couple then, counting every penny.

'So what did they decide?' enquired Sloan with genuine interest. Murder case this might be but where the Superintendent was concerned there were always moments to savour for recounting afterwards among friends in the canteen, too.

'Leeyes proposed we used Rule 13-4: "Accidentally moving loose impediment",' replied the Secretary.

'He did, did he?' said Sloan, straight-faced. The Superintendent had an infinite capacity to complicate any situation.

By the window, Detective Constable Crosby opened his mouth to say something, thought better of it, and closed it again.

'But the Captain didn't think it applied,' said Pursglove.

'That's golfing for you,' said Sloan.

English law wasn't codified. Theoretically you could do what you liked unless there was a specific law against it. Obviously not so, golf. He must remember to stress the downside of the game to his wife. This included learning the rules.

'We decided instead to deem the entire sixth hole out of bounds,' said the Secretary. 'There is provision for that in the Rules.'

Sloan nodded. The sixth hole had the makings of a hazard for a detective inspector, too, but in a different way: a stumbling block in a career path, unless the case was solved speedily.

'And we have a Local Rule that the practice hole can be substituted when another hole is deemed temporarily unplayable for any reason,' explained Alan Pursglove. 'Only in competitions, mind you. Not in Medal play, you understand.'

Detective Inspector Sloan, rosarian par excellence, did not understand. All he really understood was that the Rule Book was the Code Napoleon of the game.

'So that means that we can get players back out on the course without delay,' said Pursglove.

'Which of the Ten Commandments is that?' enquired Detective Constable Crosby subversively.

'A Golf Club Secretary shall not be a fool,' came back Pursglove briskly. 'Now, gentlemen, unless there's anything else...'

'You've got to hand it to these golfers,' said Crosby as the Secretary went out. 'Kick one of them and they all limp.'

'A word, miss, if we may.'

Detective Inspector Sloan and Woman Sergeant Perkins had caught up with Hilary Trumper just after Sloan had dispatched Crosby to interview the greenkeeper. The girl was heading back towards the caddies' hut but seemed in no hurry to get there.

'What about?' she said truculently, coming to a halt on the grass.

'Matthew Steele,' said Sloan. Close-up, he realised the girl was younger than he'd first thought.

'What about him?' she asked, catching her breath suddenly.

'Can you tell us where he is?'

'Oh, safely on his way to Lasserta,' she said, quickly recovering her composure. 'In a train, actually. He was going overland for the experience. It's a long way,' she added unnecessarily.

'When did you last see him?'

'Tuesday.'

'Where?'

'At home.' She faltered. 'I don't usually come up here.'

'Whose home?'

'Oh, mine, or rather, my parents',' she said lightly. 'He hasn't got one. At least, not what you'd call a home. He shares his college digs with a crowd.'

'Not private,' nodded Sloan.

Sergeant Polly Perkins came to life and said in a friendly way 'Your mother and father like him then?'

'Oh, yes,' she said tepidly. 'Mother particularly.'

Polly Perkins did her wise-woman party piece. 'Fathers seldom like the young men their daughters bring home the first time they come.'

Hilary Trumper flashed her a grateful look. 'You're right there.'

'Fathers tend to see daughters as their little girls for a lot longer than they really are,' said Sergeant Perkins with every appearance of sympathy, suppressing all mention of those fathers whom she had come across in her work who had assumed little girls to be much older than they really were.

And gone to prison for it.

'They don't believe that these days we've got minds of our own,' said the girl fiercely.

Sergeant Perkins was a model of empathy. 'They do find it difficult.'

'And to make it worse,' said Hilary Trumper, clearly aggrieved, 'Daddy hasn't a lot of time for economists.'

As far as Sloan was concerned, Trumper *père* was not the only one who didn't have a lot of time for economists.

'He's a proper businessman, you see,' said the girl, quite unconscious of the non sequitur.

Neither of the police present needed telling that. Trumper and Trumper's vehicles were everywhere in the county.

'Is he a golfer, too?' asked Sloan.

'Yes and no.'

'Which?' asked Sloan. Yes or no was the more usual mode in the police way of questioning.

'Yes, he belongs,' she said, sulkily, 'but no he doesn't play much. And he only belongs,' she added, 'so that he knows what's going on and can pick up business in the Clubhouse.'

'I don't suppose he's the only one,' said Sloan.

'It's here that he met Matt,' she volunteered. 'He caddied for him once and then I met Matt one day when I came up to collect Dad.' She fixed the policeman with a defiant look. 'Because of not drinking and driving.'

'Much safer,' said Sloan. 'Talking of which, why did you use the word "safely" just then when you were talking about your friend Matt?'

'Did I?' she flashed him a disarming smile. 'I didn't mean to. Matthew must be halfway there by now.'

'So why are you here now, miss, when he isn't?'

'I'm finding out all I can about the game while he's away,' she said, 'so that we can play together when he gets back.' She set her jaw. 'I'm going to surprise him with my grasp of it.'

'How long is he going to be abroad?' asked Sloan. He would have to look up Lasserta in his atlas.

'Most of the academic year,' sighed the girl. 'It's part of his course.'

'That's a long time when you're young,' said Sergeant

Perkins kindly.

'Very,' she said. 'But these days it's not so bad because we can keep in touch quite easily.'

'By telephone?' said Sloan.

'By text message,' she said in a way that was meant to make Sloan feel old.

And did.

'Every day – that's all the while he can charge up his mobile, of course. He said it might be difficult sometimes while he was travelling.'

'These messages,' said Sloan.

'Yes?' The breathlessness in her voice had come back.

'Have you stored them?'

She flushed. 'Well, yes…why shouldn't I?'

'Might we see them?'

Sloan watched the blood drain out of her face as she fumbled in her pocket for her mobile and automatically noted that the hand that offered it to him had a tremor that hadn't been there before.

Chapter Twelve

'Nasty attack of the squitters,' said a whey-faced Joe Briggs, greenkeeper. He was still moving with the extreme caution common to those who have been recently ill. 'Don't know what brought it on.'

'If you ask me,' said his wife, 'it was that pork pie.'

'Can't have been,' said the man flatly. 'We all ate that and no one else has been ill.'

'We must be grateful for small mercies, then, mustn't we?' His wife turned to Detective Constable Crosby who, being unmarried, had been observing the enactment of this domestic exchange with detachment. 'I've never seen anything like it,' she said.

Joe Briggs stirred uneasily.

'Couldn't stop going,' said his wife graphically. 'No sooner was he back in his chair than he was back on the…'

The greenkeeper waved a hand and essayed a weak smile. 'I think they call it Montezuma's Revenge…'

'Or Delhi Belly,' said Crosby, who has never been farther afield than Calais and that only for the day.

'I don't hold with foreign food,' said Mrs Briggs.

The greenkeeper summoned up some reserve of strength from somewhere to protest. 'We didn't have any foreign food.'

'That's as may be,' said his wife. She rounded on Crosby. 'What I want to know is when he'll be fit to go back to work. Can't have him sitting here all day.'

'What did the doctor say?' countered Crosby.

She sniffed. 'Gave him something to stop the runs but it didn't, did it, Joe?'

'No,' he agreed wanly.

'And told you to drink a lot,' she said, 'but you didn't, did you?'

'Didn't feel much liking drinking anything,' he admitted. 'Afraid of being sick if I did.'

'Nasty,' said Crosby. 'When did it come on?'

'Middle of the week,' said Mrs Briggs before the man could speak.

'Wednesday,' he said. 'I know it was Wednesday because Thursdays and Fridays I always keep free to cut the greens for Saturdays and Sundays and I couldn't possibly get myself there. Not nohow.'

'He worried about that,' said his wife, 'but as I told Mr Pursglove, Joe couldn't even stand for long let alone push those great big mowers about.'

'I don't push them,' protested Joe Briggs. 'They're diesel driven.'

Both Detective Constable Crosby and Mrs Briggs dismissed this as irrelevant.

'So was it Wednesday that you had the pork pie?' asked Crosby.

'Tuesday night,' said his wife for him.

'What did you have Tuesday while you were at work?' asked the Detective Constable.

'What I always have,' replied the man pallidly. 'Sandwiches.'

'There was nothing wrong with his sandwiches,' said Mrs Briggs, bridling.

'I put them up myself. Sardine, they were.'

Joe winced visibly at the mention of food.

'And where were they while you were out on the course on Tuesday?' asked Crosby.

'In my snap-tin, like always,' replied the greenkeeper.

'And where did you leave the snap-tin then?' persisted a terrier-like Crosby.

'In my bothy,' said the greenkeeper. 'On the side, there. By my flask.'

'Like always,' said Crosby for him.

'That's right. But what's all this got to do with the police?' asked Briggs.

'Everything,' said Detective Constable Crosby with empressement. 'Or nothing,' he added fairly.

'Do you know something we don't?' demanded Mrs Briggs. 'If so, I'd like to know what it is before Joe gets any worse.'

'We don't tell people what we know,' said Crosby with dignity, 'or let them know what we don't know.'

'Great,' said Mrs Briggs sarcastically.

'It can be useful to let people worry about it a bit,' said Crosby, taking his leave.

There had been no sign of the Superintendent since he had departed hot-foot in search of the Men's Captain. Sloan himself was now established once more behind the desk in the Secretary's room instead, his notebook open at a fresh page.

He was relishing a moment's peace and quiet without Crosby when Molly from the bar knocked and put her head round the door. 'Message for you from Mrs Sloan, Inspector. She wants to know when she should expect you home.'

Sloan looked up. 'What did you tell her?' he asked with interest.

Molly gave a slow smile. 'Same as I always say when the gentlemen's wives ring up to find out where they are.'

'What's that?' he asked curiously.

'That I haven't seen them myself but that I'll tell them their wife has rung when I do.' She gave another of her slow smiles. 'There's no way round that, is there?'

'None,' said Sloan heartily. 'Molly, you're a great loss to the Diplomatic Corps.'

'Thank you, Inspector.'

'Now, have you seen Sergeant Perkins anywhere?'

'I haven't seen her myself, Inspector, but I'll tell her you're asking for her when I do.'

'I could well have left my nine iron out on the course, Inspector,' admitted Gerald Moffat. 'I'm not sure.' He looked older and more vulnerable than he had done out in the bar. He was less didactic, too. 'I'm not getting any younger, you know.'

Sloan had persuaded the man out of the Clubroom and into the Secretary's office.

'But it wasn't handed in,' said Moffat, 'and so I had to buy another.'

'I see,' said Sloan, who always allowed himself to buy another rose when one died – even though it had to go into new ground, ground that wasn't rose-sick.

'Things aren't what they were. Nothing's safe these days,' complained Moffat.

The police view – which was a longer one – was that nothing had ever been safe, but all Sloan said was 'Can you remember when you last used that particular club? It's for bunkers, isn't it?'

'And for long grass,' said Moffat. 'Get off the fairway on some holes here and you'd need it then.'

'So you'd have last used it when?' asked Sloan patiently.

'I'd have to think,' scowled Moffat. After a moment his face cleared. 'I remember. It was on the tenth about a week ago. I sliced my shot on the fairway and got in between the trees so I had to play a squeeze shot to get out. Did for my chances of the Kemberland Cup for this year, I'm afraid.'

Sloan said 'That would be one of your competitions, I take it?'

Moffat nodded. 'You'll have seen some of the Cups over the mantelpiece in the Clubroom, Inspector.'

He could hardly have missed them. Or the reinforced glass

cabinet full of other silver cups, salvers and trophies. They didn't have any of those at the Police Station. The victories over there were recorded in prison sentences, in a public protected from crime, and in the maintenance of a state in which law and order prevailed. Achieved but not rewarded with silver ornaments, those successes. Their failures, on the other hand, were writ large in newspaper headlines.

Sloan tried another tack. 'When did you realise that you'd lost it?'

'Oh, that's easy.' He let out an involuntary sigh. 'Yesterday. I was playing the short fifteenth and overshot the green.' He gave the policeman a sharp look. '"Never up, never in", you know.'

Sloan didn't know.

'Got in the rough – dead in line, though – but much too far behind the pin. Thought I'd try a squeeze shot with a bit of spin to hold it on the green and then I found the damn club wasn't there.'

'So?'

'Had to take a five iron instead. Not the same thing at all. A really open face is what you want there. Lost the hole, of course.'

Sloan began to see why golf has been so famously described as a good walk spoilt.

'I was one down at the fourteenth so naturally it was important,' carried on Moffat.

So was finding out who it was who had killed the young man in the bunker at the sixth. 'Of course,' murmured Sloan trying to sound sympathetic at this cruel turn of fate for the golfer. The cruel turn of fate of the murder victim was what was really on his mind. He didn't alter his tone because one of the lessons that had been dinned into him by that peerless mentor, his first Station Sergeant, had been always to agree with an interviewee whenever you could. "Lulls 'em into a false sense of security," he'd been wont to say before charging a suspect.

Sloan was fairly sure that Gerald Moffat wasn't a suspect: only that someone had wanted him to be, which was very different. 'Did the club do the trick for you when you last used it?' he asked Moffat with every appearance of interest.

'That day on the tenth?' he said. 'I'm afraid not. Eric Simmonds beat me in the Kemberland Cup but he's been ill ever since and had to give his next opponent a walkover.'

'So, sir, I reckon it wasn't food poisoning that made the green-keeper ill.' Detective Constable Crosby was reporting back to the Clubhouse.

'Someone wanted him out of the way,' pronounced Sloan mordantly.

'While they borrowed his truck to take the body over to the sixth,' said Crosby. The truck was something that rankled with Crosby. He didn't like walking.

'While they dug a hole,' said Sloan.

'That reminds me, Crosby, very soon we must have a little chat with this man who comes in at night.' He flipped over the pages of his notebook. 'Bobby Curd. Find out where he lives, will you? And let me have the results of the DNA tests on the truck as soon as they come back...'

'May I come in?' Police Sergeant Perkins put her head round the door of the Secretary's office. She was bearing a tray loaded with man-sized brown rolls.

'Tummy time,' pronounced Crosby eagerly.

'Technically I think we're off-duty while we eat and eat we must,' said the policewoman. She pointed to the food and said doubtfully 'I hope I've chosen the right things for you two. It wasn't easy.'

'We're not fussy,' said Sloan.

'Only hungry,' said Crosby.

'I didn't mean that,' she said. 'It's their menu. It's all in golf lingo. They call this little lot an "eagle" and it's an "albatross" if you have a hard-boiled egg with it.'

Crosby said 'As long as it'll go down red lane, it's all right with me...'

'Gammon's a "slice",' said Polly Perkins, 'and "shank" is cold roast lamb.'

'Well, I never,' said Crosby between mouthfuls.

'It doesn't matter what it's called,' said Detective Inspector Sloan, taking a bite. 'It's good.'

'Cheese is a "wedge", whatever that might be,' said Polly Perkins, 'and chicken is...'

'We'll never guess,' said Sloan ironically.

'"Birdie"?' suggested Crosby insouciantly.

Polly Perkins favoured the Constable with a long look before she said 'And orange juice is a "squeeze". Me, I'd rather call a spade a spade any day.'

'Me too,' said Sloan. 'So we can call this case a ...'

'Balls-up?' suggested Crosby.

'A matter of motive,' said Sloan coldly. 'That is, we know how the victim was killed, where he was buried, and probably when.'

'But not why,' agreed Sergeant Perkins.

'Or who he is,' pointed out Crosby.

'Or where he was killed,' concurred Sloan. 'All of which we shall need to know.'

'All in good time,' said Police Sergeant Perkins. Time was a great healer in domestics. So was a spell in a cell.

'Anyone want that beef roll?' asked Crosby.

'There's a lot to be done,' persisted Sloan. 'There's the locker room to be searched for a club and a pair of shoes for starters.'

'Even though we don't know if they're there,' said Crosby, his mouth full.

'And we need to talk to the Planning people at the Council about this new development.'

'Do people kill for planning permission?' enquired Sergeant Perkins with the detached interest of one who spent most of her time among those without much in the way of possessions.

'They kill for money, which comes to the same thing,' said Sloan.

'True.' She stretched out her hand for another roll. 'What about business? Do they kill for that?'

'That's money, too,' said Sloan.

'Gilchrists' is in trouble,' she informed them. 'The word on the street is that they're laying men off as quietly as they can. And women.'

'Going for broke?' enquired Crosby.

'Short of work,' said Sergeant Perkins.

'So this development job with the Golf Club would be important to them,' mused Sloan.

'It doesn't exactly sound like chicken feed to me,' said the policewoman. 'And I'm not in business, thank goodness.' She took another bite at her roll. 'At least, not in that sort of business.'

'I should have thought any firm would be glad to get their hands on this contract,' said Sloan.

'There'll be wheels within wheels, though,' said Polly Perkins enigmatically. 'There always are.'

They were interrupted by a knock on the door of the Secretary's office. 'It's Molly from the bar,' said the woman who came in. 'There's a man outside asking for a Detective Inspector Sloan.'

'Coming.' Sloan uncoiled himself from the desk, casting a regretful glance at the last remaining roll on the plate.

The policeman outside had come post haste straight from the dentist's. 'You know the one, I mean, sir. His surgery's down by the bridge.'

'I know. And?'

The policeman produced a message sheet and handed it over to Sloan. The message on it was duly signed and quite unequivocal – but no surprise. It stated that the details of the dentition sent over from the mortuary corresponded in every particular with the dental records on the chart of Matthew Steele, aged twenty, kept by the dentist.

As Detective Inspector Sloan walked back towards the Secretary's room, an odd phrase came into his mind. He'd first heard it when insinuating himself between the Calleford Hunt and the hunt saboteurs.

Both groups had been on the point of calling it a day when the hunt had had what they called "a three o'clock fox". Horses, hounds, hunters, saboteurs and policemen had all set off in a great hurry in a totally new direction.

He put his hand on the door and went back into their temporary headquarters. The plate of rolls was empty. But it was Polly Perkins who had the last one in her hand.

Hilary Trumper made her way back to the caddies' shed, her shoulders drooping ever so slightly now.

'I've seen the professional,' she said to Dickie Castle, 'like you said.'

'It's a start, miss,' said Dickie.

'And he's going to take me round first.'

'But, Hilary...' Edmund Pemberton started to say something.

'That's right,' Dickie chopped him off. 'Show you the ropes himself.'

'Our Jock Selkirk knows his way around, if anyone does,' said Bert Hedges blandly.

The girl shot him a scathing look. 'I know my way around, too.'

'I'm sure you do, miss,' said Bert Hedges, dodging an imaginary blow, 'but it's as well to have an expert show you.'

'Tell me,' she said, looking round, 'who did Matthew take around most?'

'Matt? Oh, he'd go out with anyone who wanted a caddy,' said Bert.

'Not backward about coming forward,' agreed Dickie.

'Matt was never one of your Right Royal Hangbacks,' said Bert.

'Who were they?' Hilary Trumper looked both puzzled and curious.

So did Edmund Pemberton. 'I've never heard of them but Hilary...'

'You're too young,' said Dickie swiftly.

'They're the troops that didn't quite get into action but came back with those who had done and got patted on the back just like they did,' said Bert, veteran.

'So there wasn't anyone special Matt liked to go out with then?' persisted the girl.

'Let's see now, miss.' Dickie Castle at least took the question seriously. 'He went out with Mr Garwood for the third round of the Clarembald Cup.'

'Who beat Peter Gilchrist,' said Bert.

'Or to put it another way,' said Bert Hedges pithily, 'Peter Gilchrist didn't have a caddy and lost.'

'Who else did he caddy for?' asked Hilary Trumper.

'I know he took Major Bligh out one day and he caddied for that old fuss-pot Moffat for his round of the Kemberland Cup,' said Dickie Castle. 'Because nobody else wanted to,' he added gratuitously.

'Anyone else?' she asked.

Bert Hedges wrinkled his nose at the apparent effort of remembering. 'I think he went out when Brian Southon and Peter Gilchrist played their round in the Pletchford Plate but I don't know which of 'em he was caddying for.'

'Gilchrist,' supplied Dickie Castle.

'He lost.'

'Off his game, I daresay,' said Bert Hedges largely. 'He must have a lot on his mind and you can't play good golf with something on your mind.'

'You can't play good golf with anything on your mind,' said Dickie Castle, low handicap player, seriously.

'I suppose you remember all the matches and who won them?' said Hilary.

Dickie Castle said carefully 'Not always, miss.'

'Hilary,' began Pemberton again, 'I think you need to...'

'We've sort of had to bring it to mind lately,' explained Bert Hedges. He glanced at Edmund Pemberton. 'Haven't we, young Ginger?'

Pemberton said 'I keep trying to tell Hilary...'

Bert Hedges said 'Because we've just had the police in here

asking exactly the same question.'

'They were looking for you, too, miss,' said Dickie Castle. 'Asked us if we knew where to find you.'

Edmund Pemberton was just in time to catch Hilary Trumper as her face paled and she slid to the floor.

'Who?' bellowed the Superintendent.

'Matthew Robert Steele,' repeated Detective Inspector Sloan patiently.

'One of the caddies?'

'Him. Last seen on the course late last Tuesday afternoon after he got back from caddying for Gerald Moffat.'

'And said, wasn't he,' Leeyes sounded flinty, 'to be on his way to some benighted foreign country or another?'

'Lasserta, sir.'

Since Leeyes considered all foreign countries to be benighted, he ignored this. 'But I thought you said that that girl Hilary Trumper had been having text messages from him.'

'She said she had,' said Sloan cautiously. 'She might have had.'

'You mean, I take it, that someone else might have been sending them,' boomed Superintendent Leeyes, unwilling as ever to believe that distance didn't affect the volume of his telephone.

'There was no mobile phone buried with or near the deceased,' said Sloan patiently. He wondered idly if anyone had been buried with their mobile telephone. One of them as grave goods might be a considerable help to archaeologists in future – after the next Armageddon, perhaps.

Leeyes grunted.

'It's not like recognising a voice or handwriting...' went on Sloan. He wasn't sure of the legal status of a text message stored in the memory of a mobile telephone, although there would be bound to be legal eager-beavers somewhere out there arguing about it and lusting after test cases.

'I didn't suppose it was,' snapped Leeyes, an unwilling late-comer to modern communications technology.

'And text messages are what you might called stylised, sir. I mean,' he said, elaborating this, 'for instance I understand the letters IOU mean "I love you".'

'In my young days,' thundered Leeyes, 'those letters meant that you owed somebody something and had promised to pay them.'

'Things,' said Sloan delicately, 'aren't what they were.' Debts weren't what they were either: drug-users couldn't pay for their habit with promissory notes – at least not for long.

'These messages, Sloan, have you checked them yourself?'

'No, sir.' He coughed. 'I thought it more appropriate that the girl's – er – instrument should be dealt with by someone more into that sort of thing.' That there were forensic mobile-tele-phone specialists was just another sign of the march of progress. It hadn't been like that when Sloan had been on the beat.

Leeyes grunted again.

'The girl insists that she didn't have any doubts about the authenticity of the messages,' said Sloan.

'Did he say anything about where he was that would prove it?' Nobody could say that the Superintendent didn't have an eye for essentials.

'Only that the trip was GR8.'

'And what might that mean?'

'It's text-speak for "great",' Sloan hurried on, 'but she did agree there was nothing unexpected in them except…'

'Except?'

'Apparently this fellow always used to sign off with TTFN.'

'And what, pray, might that mean? I'm not into reading the runes, you know.'

'Ta ta for now.'

'And?'

'These messages finish with CU.'

'Let me guess,' said Leeyes, heavily patient.

'It stands for "See you",' said Sloan unwillingly.

'And that was there instead?'

'Yes, sir.'

'But she isn't going to be seen by him? That it, Sloan?'

'Not now, sir.'

Detective Inspector Sloan was still sitting in the Secretary's room when Crosby came in.

'Your wife rang, sir,' he said.

'And?'

'She wanted to know if you had all the clothes you needed with you.'

'Ring her back, will you, Crosby, and say I've got everything I need for the time being, thank you.' Like any good golfer, he would need to improve his lie – and soon. This was no time for playing word games with anyone, least of all his wife. Tempting as it was to lead her on, he must desist...

And think.

He sat at the Secretary's desk, his notebook in front of him. He turned over a new page but the paper, a reproach of virgin whiteness, remained blank. He wasn't ready to put pen to paper yet.

Instead he stared out of the window on to the course. The view was made up of a symphony of shades of green. There was the lush fairway, shading off to degrees of rough, deeper-coloured grass, all leading the eye in the direction of a putting green of billiard-table smoothness, the whole surrounded by a careful composition of trees. That it should be the resting place of a murdered young man seemed all wrong – not only an offence against the Queen's Peace but against Nature, too.

Nature, though, he reminded himself, starting to doodle

absently on the paper, might be beautiful but could be – was – unkind. No, not unkind, merely indifferent…and indifference was something that wasn't in the police canon.

This philosophical train of thought was interrupted by Detective Constable Crosby's coming back to the little office. 'Mrs Sloan said to say thank you for your message, sir, and that she was looking forward to seeing you later.'

'Right, now sit down and take some notes.' He would have to formulate a plan of action before the Superintendent got on to him again.

'Yes, sir.' Since the only other chair in the room was piled high with papers, Crosby stood first on one foot and then on the other in front of one of the large charts on every wall on which the names of the winner repeatedly advanced across the sheet, the names of losers falling away as they were defeated and thus out of the competition.

The Constable put his finger up to the nearest of them, tracing a name along a stepped path not unlike a pyramid lying on its side. 'The winner doesn't half have to beat a lot of people to get to the end,' he remarked.

'Life's like that,' said Sloan.

'These cups, sir, that they get for winning…'

'What about them?'

'Are they worth anything?'

'Not a life,' said Sloan soberly, 'if that's what you're getting at, Crosby. In fact, from what I've seen of them they're not worth anything much in themselves either.'

'Well, then…'

'Rogues don't usually bother with them because of the engraving but it's the names on them that are important to the winners. You must remember that.'

'But it's only for a year,' protested the Constable, 'that's if those boards in the bar are anything to go by.'

'Think of them as trophies,' said Sloan, drawing another

meaningless sketch in his notebook. 'Taken home with your name on it and put on the mantelpiece for a year. A feather in your cap...' Feathers in police caps weren't meant to be visible to the world at large: and that in his view included not standing on the courtroom steps boasting.

'But having to be fought for all over again next time?' said Crosby.

'Life's like that, too,' said Sloan.

'Something must have been worth killing a man for,' said Crosby.

'Something must have *seemed* worth killing a man for,' Sloan corrected him.

'What we have to do is work out what it might have been now that we know the name of the victim.'

'Where does the girl come in, sir?'

'And why does she come in to the Club just now?' countered Sloan. 'She's not a member, she doesn't play, and she suddenly wants to caddy for anyone and everyone.'

'Her father's a member and he plays.'

'I'm told Luke Trumper is what you might call a business member,' said Sloan.

'The Secretary tells me he picks up a good bit of work in the bar but that he's not into playing much.'

'This development...'

'Good thinking, Crosby. According to Alan Pursglove, Trumpers are one of the firms sniffing round for the contract.' Sloan started a little list on his pad.

'So is Peter Gilchrist...oh, and United Mellemetics in the person of their Nigel Halesworth. He plays here, too. Pursglove didn't mention Calleshire Consolidated but I expect they'll be interested, too.'

'So it must be worth something,' said the Constable. 'United Mellemetics don't go in for chicken feed.'

'Oh, yes, Crosby, it'll be worth quite a lot – especially to

Peter Gilchrist's outfit.' He tapped his notebook with his waterproof pencil. 'But Calleshire businessmen don't usually go around knocking off their caddies for trade purposes.'

'Perhaps Matthew Steele knew something we don't,' suggested Crosby dubiously.

'Or something that they don't,' said Sloan.

'Or got in the way.'

'Somebody must have thought they'd be better off without him,' agreed Sloan tacitly. He sat up straight and assumed a dictating mode. 'Now, Crosby, this is what has to be done...'

Molly from the bar put her head round the door again. 'I've come for the tray,' she said, adding tactfully, 'your Superintendent's just finishing his meal, out there, too.'

Detective Inspector Sloan said 'If he asks for me, Molly, say we're following up a lead, will you?' He stood up. 'Let's go, Crosby.'

'Yes, sir,' said Crosby with alacrity. The Constable was not averse to going anywhere provided it was on wheels: four wheels. He had no great love for any other form of transport and none whatsoever for walking. 'Where to, sir?'

Sloan turned back a page in his notebook. 'Rose Cottage, Deep Lane, Cullingoak.'

'Sounds a nice address.'

It wasn't. Not one that the water-colourist Helen Allingham would have wanted to paint, anyway. Whilst there might once have been hollyhocks lining the path and roses round the cottage door there certainly weren't now. True, there was a very overgrown rambler sprawled over the fence in front of the cottage but it had the same uncared-for look as the rest of the property. Somewhere a dog was barking.

In fact the outside appearance of Bobby Curd's dwelling was singularly unattractive. For one thing it comprised a tiny cottage with all manner of outhouses, sheds and a deplorable lean-to abutting it. At the bottom of what might have once been a small garden was a round little brick building which, whatever it was used for now, patently had been there before the advent of main drainage. Less than clean curtains hung in the windows.

'Lacks the woman's touch, wouldn't you say, sir?' said Crosby, clambering out of the police car and looking at the peeling paint.

'Lacks any touch,' said Sloan crisply. 'Or any roses to speak of,' he added, looking round.

Their speech provoked a further outbreak of barking from an unseen dog.

'Come along,' said Sloan. 'Let's see what Bobby Curd can tell us about the course at night.'

The only response to their knocking was another outbreak of barking. They could hear the dog scratching and snarling on the other side of the door but no one came to open the door.

'Try the latch,' ordered Sloan.

'It sounds a big dog,' said the Constable.

'I expect it is,' said Sloan. 'That's if its dish over there is anything to go by.'

Crosby regarded a sizeable bowl with misgiving. He braced his shoulders back and advanced on the door, calling out 'Good dog...'

It was.

A large lurcher was standing sentinel over a dead body that was lying behind the door: a dead body with a fearsome head wound.

In a dry summer large boughs of oak are subject to a phenomenon called "sudden branch drop". To Detective Inspector Sloan, gardener, looking at the dead body in front of them with its fatal head wound it looked more of a case of "sudden tree drop" than mere branch.

The gardening analogy remained in the forefront of his mind as a few lines of verse from one of his old horticultural books welled up from somewhere in his memory.

He quoted it softly now, almost under his breath:

'Little Herb Robert,
Bright and small,
Peeps from the bank,
And the stone wall.'

'Sorry, sir,' said Crosby. 'I didn't quite catch that.'

As the two policemen peered down at the crumpled form that was lying at the bottom of the staircase, still defended by the dog, Detective Inspector Sloan said 'That would have been his trouble.'

'What would?' asked Crosby.

'Seeing too much.'

At the Berebury Golf Club all the action was in the locker rooms. Police Sergeant Polly Perkins was leading the search in the Ladies' Section.

'All the lockers?' the Lady Captain asked, eyebrows raised.

'And all their golf bags,' said Polly Perkins.

'You're looking for something,' concluded the Lady Captain, giving an involuntary shiver.

'We are,' said the policewoman. 'We'd like each member here to confirm that there are the correct number of clubs in their bags and to identify their own shoes.'

The Lady Captain frowned. 'That'll take time.'

'In a murder investigation,' said Police Sergeant Polly Perkins magisterially, 'time is immaterial.'

Matters were not proceeding quite so smoothly in the men's locker rooms where Superintendent Leeyes, unable immediately to locate Sloan, had decided to supervise the operation himself. This was not a help.

'We'll start with all the men up here today,' he announced to two hapless Constables brought in at short notice from foot patrol in Berebury High Street. 'Line 'em up outside the door.'

Golfers thus rounded-up hung about out round the entrance to the locker room while the Superintendent addressed them, the Captain at his side. 'You're to come in one at a time under police supervision, and check on your own golf clubs – without touching them, of course. And then identify any shoes that are yours.' He looked round at them all. 'That clearly understood?'

'So you know what you're looking for,' stated Doug Garwood reasonably.

'We do,' said Leeyes.

'And you've got some footprints, too, I suppose?' said Peter Gilchrist.

Superintendent Leeyes ignored this since it wasn't true but he didn't want to say so.

'So can we get on with it then?' asked James Hopland, whose knee always hurt more when he was standing still.

Leeyes was about to say 'All in good time' when he remembered that Hopland, although old and arthritic, remained influential in the Club – and would have a vote at the election for the Committee. He said instead with a courtesy quite alien to him 'Would you like to be first?'

'Are you looking for a particular club?' enquired Nigel Halesworth, adding with apparent inconsequence 'Mine have all got my name on them – present from the firm, you know, for twenty-five years' hard work.'

'We're looking for any club in your bag that shouldn't be there,' said Leeyes blandly. 'And we'd like you to just identify your own shoes, that's all. Not handle them.'

As a process it was slow, tedious and at first from a police point of view, unrewarding. But not uninteresting. Some lockers proved to be storing that for which they were not really intended. This included a bottle of rum.

'For cold days,' said its owner. 'Put it back.'

There was a gift-wrapped parcel in the next.

'The wife's birthday present. It's the only place she can't get to.'

A set of woman's clothes…

'No, of course, they're not mine,' spluttered a man to the police. 'They're the girlfriend's.'

A teddy bear.

'A sort of mascot,' explained another man, blushing deeply. 'I pat him before I go out.'

A medallion of St Andrew.

'Patron saint of golfers,' said the man in whose locker this was hanging. 'Must be, mustn't he?'

The only real action came when it was Brian Southon's turn to open his locker.

Under Superintendent Leeyes' eagle eye, he peered into his golf bag, saying 'There should be two woods, eleven irons and a putter...hullo...'

'Two woods, twelve irons and a putter,' said Leeyes, putting up a beefy hand to stop Southon going any nearer. 'Just tell me which is the one that shouldn't be there.'

'There are two nine irons in my bag,' said Brian Southon hollowly. 'One isn't mine. Look,' he said eagerly, advancing towards the bag, 'It doesn't match the others, does it? You can see that for yourself, can't you?'

'Don't touch,' said Leeyes at his most authoritarian. 'Just point and tell me what you see.'

Southon swallowed. 'A number-nine iron from someone else's set. Must be. Besides you aren't allowed to carry more than fourteen clubs. Against the Rules. Everyone knows that.'

'And how long might it have been there?' asked Leeyes, never one to answer a witness's question.

'Search me,' said Brian Southon. He grimaced. 'Sorry, I didn't mean that. I meant, I don't know, do I, or I'd have handed it in.'

'When were you last in a bunker?' asked Leeyes.

Southon rocked back on his heels and said wildly 'I'd have to think...no, I remember now. It was on Sunday morning and I'd started shanking and ended up in the bad bunker at the sixth.'

'What did you get out with?' asked Leeyes.

'My number nine.' He looked at the policeman and said with unmistakable emphasis. 'My own number nine.'

'And was this extra club in your bag then?' enquired Leeyes.

Brian Southon looked shaken. 'I couldn't swear that it was...'

'Pity,' said Leeyes.

'Or wasn't.'

'You may have to swear to just that, then,' said Leeyes helpfully.

When most people talked abut the full panoply of the law what they usually had in mind was a red-robed judge sitting in oak-panelled splendour under a Royal Coat of Arms set within some ancient and imposing building in the middle of a County town. All and sundry would be present in their best formal dress and definitely on their best behaviour – especially the accused.

The full panoply of the law invoked by Detective Inspector Sloan now at Rose Cottage was more mundane – but just as necessary at the very beginning of the long process of justice as at its culmination. For the second time that day he called out a series of specialists in the technical aspects of the detection of murder – the Scenes of Crime Officers, the police photographers, the fingerprint experts, that arcane species, the DNA technician – new but now vital in almost every investigation – and the consultant pathologist.

'And there's nothing for it, Crosby,' Sloan said with the greatest reluctance, 'but I'm afraid we're going to have to hold a press conference, too.'

'What are we going to do about the dog, sir?' asked Crosby, eyeing the animal warily.

'I think you'd better take it into protective custody,' he said. Protective custody was what he always felt he needed when confronted by the press. 'It's not going to let anyone near the deceased.'

'It is a trifle defensive, sir,' said Crosby, making no move in the direction of the dog.

Sloan sighed. A police dog-handler would have to be added to the long list of those summoned to Rose Cottage. 'All right, Crosby. Let's see what we can see.'

They moved carefully through the cottage, making for the kitchen. An open milk bottle stood on the table, the milk turbid and noisome.

Crosby wrinkled his nose in distaste.

'Might give us a time of death,' said Sloan. 'I daresay the neighbours are so used to turning a blind eye to his comings and goings that they're not going to tell us much.'

Crosby pointed to a slice of bread, already mouldy. 'Doesn't look the sort you'd step round and borrow half a cup of sugar from. Look, sir, the back door's open.'

'The exit strategy of whoever did this,' said Sloan. Burglars always established an escape route: so did murderers.

'Easiest thing in the world to nip inside and up the stairs…'

'And get the old chap from above and behind,' finished Sloan bleakly, 'before walking out again.'

'Though why the dog didn't bark…'

'One of the other reasons why dogs don't bark in the night, Crosby, is that they have been doped. Make sure that this dog's bowl goes to Forensics.'

'It's wide enough awake now,' said Crosby, still keeping his distance from the animal. 'And hungry.'

'If the dog's dinner has been doped,' said Sloan, thinking aloud, 'it presupposes a fair degree of malice aforethought, not that I think there's anything fortuitous about any of this.'

'It might not like me taking his dish away,' said Crosby, still eyeing the dog.

'True,' said Sloan, 'but get on with it all the same. We've work to do.'

'I suppose,' said Crosby, anxious to postpone approaching what was left of the dog's dinner, 'what this old boy saw was someone on the course at night digging a grave for Matthew Steele…'

'And what I suppose,' said Detective Inspector Sloan, 'is

that he was unwise enough to apprise whoever it was that he had seen of that very fact.'

'Dangerous,' said Crosby.

'Foolhardy, if you ask me,' said Sloan. He turned his head and listened to the sound of a police siren getting nearer. 'Is that the cavalry I hear in the distance?'

What to do with a fainting girl had taxed the caddies more than somewhat. Their first instinct was to park her carefully on the nearest bench, her back firmly against the wall and her head sunk down between her knees.

'Are you all right?' asked Bert Hedges solicitously.

Hilary Trumper lifted her head briefly, disclosing a face devoid of colour. She lowered her head again with a despairing moan. She looked a good deal less than all right to the men there, who immediately produced a variety of flasks and offered their contents to the girl.

Hilary Trumper waved them away with a deep sigh. 'I'll be all right in a minute.'

Bert Castle suggested that they took her over to the Ladies' Clubroom.

'No, no,' protested Hilary. 'Tell me,' she said urgently, 'what did you tell the police?'

'All we could remember about who he went out with,' said Hedges.

'I need to know, too,' she said, struggling to sit up. 'Did they say why they wanted to know about Matt?'

It is a common misconception that there is a good way to break bad news. It is equally true on the other hand that bad news can be conveyed without words. There was a concerted shuffling of feet and a universal unwillingness to meet her eyes. And a silence broken only by the odd cough.

In the end it was Edmund Pemberton who spoke first.

'No, they didn't. Not exactly.' he looked round at the

assembled men. 'But we sort of worked it out, didn't we?'

There were sounds that might have signified assent.

The girl lifted her head again.

'So?'

'They say,' murmured Pemberton unwillingly, 'that the bo...that whoever they've found at the sixth could be...that is, it's thought to be a man of about twenty.'

There had been a little more colour in her face but it drained away again as she licked dry lips and asked 'How long had it been there?'

Pemberton lowered his own head. 'They say about a week.'

He couldn't see her face now. It was back between her knees. He bent his head alongside hers. 'I think I'd better take you home, Hilary.'

That brought her upright, eyes blazing, two bright red spots coming into her cheeks. 'I'm not going home,' she said fiercely. 'Ever.'

'That you, Sloan?' barked Superintendent Leeyes down the phone. 'Where on earth have you been?'

'Berebury, at Rose Cottage...'

'Look here, we've found Moffat's club.'

'We've found Bobby Curd...' began Sloan.

'In Brian Southon's bag in the locker room here.'

'Dead,' said Sloan.

'What?' exploded the Superintendent.

'Very dead,' said Sloan firmly.

There was an uncharacteristic silence at the other end of the telephone line. It equated with the sound of cogitation on the Superintendent's part.

'I don't think, Sloan,' said Leeyes eventually, 'that we're going to find who killed Matthew Steele until we know exactly why he was murdered. Or Bobby Curd.'

'Bobby Curd, though, must have seen something,' said Sloan. 'Stands out a mile.'

'Or seen someone,' said Leeyes.

'Probably the night Steele was buried. But as to why Steele was killed, sir, I'm afraid we're no further forward.'

'Though Luke Trumper wasn't happy about the fellow pursuing his daughter.'

'Fathers seldom are – rich fathers, anyway,' said Sloan. He didn't have a daughter.

'Girls can be very wilful,' said Leeyes, who did have a daughter.

'I'm sure, sir.' It was widely supposed at the Police Station that Superintendent Leeyes was henpecked: mostly on the grounds that it explained his behaviour at work. Perhaps he was chicken-pecked as well. 'We're going to interview Luke Trumper as soon as possible.' He coughed. 'They do say, sir, that he's been up here a lot lately. Much more than usual for him, anyway.'

'Thought Steele was too young for a son-in-law, I expect,' said Leeyes sagely. 'No prospects, either...'

That wasn't what Sergeant Perkins had reported to Sloan: the prospects might have been altogether too rosy for Trumper *père's* liking.

'Some fathers, of course,' pronounced Leeyes weightily, 'will go to any lengths to stop their daughters getting mixed up with unsuitable young men.'

'Not murder, surely?' murmured Sloan, although he didn't envy the suitors, if any, of the Superintendent's daughter.

'There was that old fellow who saw his daughter drown when he wouldn't let her marry her lover,' said Leeyes.

'I don't remember...'

'You know, Sloan. Everyone knows about him.'

'Sir?'

'Some Scotsman or other – I forget his name now.'

'Really, sir?'

'A Lord, if I remember rightly.'

'I can't say that I...'

'You remember, Sloan. The girl who didn't mind the weather but who couldn't cope with an angry father. So she and her lover set off across the loch and were drowned before his eyes.'

'Loch Ullin's daughter,' faltered Sloan. He'd forgotten the winter that the Superintendent had attended classes on "Poetry and Prose". Something his superior had heard there must have stuck.

'That's the man. The other fellow was Lord of Ulva's Isle or something. Much good it did him, either.'

'It would seem, though,' said Sloan, rising to the occasion, 'that Matt Steele was no young Lochinvar. But he was sharp all the same. Very sharp from all accounts.' He hastened on. 'All we've been able to do so far, sir, is to list the golfers the deceased caddied for most recently.'

'A golfer may consider a caddy inefficient,' declared Leeyes pontifically, 'or even downright unhelpful, but not to the point of killing him out of hand.'

'Not exactly out of hand, sir,' murmured Sloan. 'These have all the hallmarks of carefully orchestrated killings.' He hesitated and then added 'By someone who knew the course well enough to recreate the pattern in the sand that had been there before and also matched that in the other bunkers.' That had been one examination, at least, that Crosby had carried out properly. 'And it wasn't the greenkeeper who did it because he was off sick.'

Somewhere at the back of his mind was the fact that he'd heard someone else at the Club had been ill, too, but the memory was elusive and he couldn't for the moment remember who it had been.

'Good thinking,' said Leeyes. 'So tell me, who was it that Steele caddied for last.'

'Peter Gilchrist.' Sloan had the answer to that ready. 'That was when Luke Trumper and Nigel Halesworth all played together in the semi-final of the Kemberland Cup.'

'That's a Stableford Competition,' said Leeyes. 'We all went out in threesomes for that.'

'Trumper won,' said Sloan, 'with thirty-three points.'

'Doesn't sound as if he had too much on his mind then,' said Leeyes thoughtfully. 'Not enough to take it off the game, anyway.'

The Superintendent might have considered that this constituted evidence. Sloan didn't and so went on 'The deceased caddied for Gilchrist, too, when he played Brian Southon in the second round of the Pletchford Plate. Gilchrist lost then, too.'

'Perhaps it was Gilchrist who had something on his mind –

oh, yes. Of course he has,' said Leeyes. 'His business. Ah, well, perhaps he'll get the contract for the work at the Club. One of them's going to. And soon. They've only got until the end of the month to get their tenders in.'

'Peter Gilchrist lost when Steele caddied for Doug Garwood, too,' said Sloan, turning over a page in his notebook. 'That was quite a while ago now.'

'Doug may be getting on but his short game's still pretty good,' opined Leeyes, golfer. 'I suppose that's what saved him.'

'Yes, sir.' Sloan flipped over another page of his notebook. 'And Steele caddied for Nigel Halesworth when he played Luke Trumper in the Matheson Trophy.'

'Trumper didn't win,' said Leeyes. 'I know because I was playing after him and saw it up on the board.'

'The curious thing about the Matheson Trophy,' said Detective Inspector Sloan, policeman, not golfer, 'is that apparently Matthew Steele bet quite a lot of money on Doug Garwood beating Peter Gilchrist in his match.'

'You mean even though Steele wasn't caddying for either of them?' enquired Superintendent Leeyes alertly.

'Yes, sir.' He cleared his throat. 'And Garwood did win and so, I suppose, in a way did Matthew Steele. His bet, anyway.' Not, he added silently to himself, that being murdered constituted winning in anyone's book.

'Gilchrist should have won,' declared Leeyes. 'He's the better player, by a long chalk although his handicap would have come into it.'

Sloan wasn't sure about golf handicaps. Down at the Police Station their handicaps comprised such things as villains and vandals, budgets and bureaucracy, traffic and traffickers…

'That would have helped Doug Garwood, would it, sir? Gilchrist's handicap.'

He heard the Superintendent blow out his cheeks in an

audible puff. 'A handicap is the imposition of special disadvantages to make a better contest...'

That wasn't how they saw their handicaps down at the Police Station but Sloan pressed on. 'So Doug Garwood would have had to concede something to Peter Gilchrist instead.'

'No, the other way round,' said Leeyes. 'Gilchrist has a lower handicap than old Doug. In his day, Doug was very good but not now he's getting on. Gilchrist would have had to give him quite a few strokes.'

'But he still lost to Garwood?'

'That,' said Leeyes, 'is what is interesting.'

'And so is how Steele knew that he would,' murmured Sloan.

'There's no question, I'm afraid,' said Leeyes, sounding unusually subdued, 'that our villain, whoever he is, will have been using local knowledge all the time.'

'It looks as if the victims were as well,' said Sloan. 'Both of them.'

'And that who ever did it was a member,' said Leeyes gloomily. 'Not good for the Club, you know, Sloan. Something like this.'

'That brings me, sir, to another thing...'

'What's that?'

'The lab people have started taking swabs for DNA identification to compare with the traces they've found on the greenkeeper's truck...and they say they'll get over to Bobby Curd's place, too, as soon as they can.'

'Quite right, Sloan.'

'From everyone at the Club, sir.'

'Naturally. We can't afford to leave anyone out at this stage. Especially Luke Trumper.'

'Exactly, sir,' said Sloan warmly. 'I knew you'd agree.'

'Well?'

'This is a bit difficult.'

'Why?'

Basely Sloan transferred the blame.

'The men in white suits want to include you, sir.'

'Me?' said Leeyes on a rising note.

'Everyone,' said Sloan. He took a deep breath. 'They've asked me to say, sir, that everyone includes you.'

Superintendent's voice hit crescendo. 'Good God, Sloan, I'm not everyone.'

'No, sir. Certainly not, sir. But, seeing you're up for the Committee they thought you'd want to set a good example.'

Helen Ewell had found her voice again. It had not reverted to normal, though, but remained high-pitched and child-like. She had found a new audience now, too, having made her way to the professional's shop. Still half in tears, she positively fell upon the man.

'Oh, Jock, it was horrible,' she cried. 'You can't imagine how horrible.'

'No,' agreed Selkirk, disentangling himself from her clasp with difficulty. 'I don't suppose I can.'

'They say it's Matt Steele, one of the caddies.' She was still clinging to him. 'That poor, poor boy. Who would do a thing like that?'

'Only a madman,' said Jock Selkirk, firmly detaching Helen's arm from his.

'And that poor girl!'

'What girl?' asked Selkirk cautiously.

'Hilary Trumper, of course. Luke's daughter.'

'Ah, I guessed she was sweet on him,' said Selkirk, slipping adroitly behind his counter out of Helen Ewell's reach.

'They say she was very attached indeed to Matt Steele.'

'A mistake,' said Selkirk dourly. 'Not her sort at all.'

Helen Ewell stood back at last and regarded the professional as if seeing him as a human being for the first time. 'What makes you say that?' she asked, her curiosity aroused.

'I know a young man on the make when I see one.'

'Oh, Jock, how can you say that about someone who's been murdered?'

'It can't do him any harm,' said the professional reasonably. 'And it's true.'

He had reckoned without Helen Ewell's womanly feelings. 'Don't you understand?' she said slowly. 'Someone's killed him here on your course.'

'I know that,' said Jock Selkirk. There was no sign now of the celebrated ladies' man nor even of the accomplished exponent of the game. Just of a very worried golf professional. 'I've had the police here today, too.'

'Here?' She looked bewildered. 'Whatever for?'

'I don't know what they came for the first time...' he began carefully.

'They've been twice, Jock? I don't understand.'

'But when they came back again they turned the place upside down.'

'But why?'

'To begin with I didn't know what they were looking for,' he said, tight-lipped. 'But what they found were a pair of shoes.'

'Shoes?' she echoed.

'Don't you understand, woman?' he said harshly. 'They found Matthew Steele's shoes here in my shop.

'In here?' She looked round the shop, totally baffled.

'No, no, not in here.' He jerked a finger over his shoulder. 'Out in my workshop at the back. In a pile of shoes waiting to have new studs fitted.'

'But...'

Jock Selkirk leaned back on his heels, ignoring her patent distress. 'Now, woman, tell me what you make of that...'

Detective Inspector Sloan carefully replaced the telephone receiver in the Secretary's office and said 'Sit down, Crosby. We need to think outside the box.'

The Constable looked at each chair in turn and chose one with the least papers on it. 'These'll have to go down on the dog shelf,' he said, stacking them carefully on the floor before taking a seat. 'Me, I thought golf was a game not a paperchase.'

'Keeping track of winners and losers takes time,' said Sloan prosaically. Theoretically, down at the Police Station they only had to keep track of the losers – or, rather, those who didn't believe in law and order. The trouble was that they weren't always the losers. Putting this engaging thought to the back of his mind for further consideration at some mythical moment when he was less busy, he pulled out his notebook. 'Let's see, where are we now?'

'Getting nowhere fast,' said Crosby dispiritedly. 'All we know for sure is who the two victims are.'

'Hardly a great leap forward, Crosby, I agree, but something to be going on with.'

Crosby jerked his shoulder in the direction of the course. 'And that the deceased's girlfriend has started to haunt the place.'

'True. Anything else?' Socrates had come to grief for asking questions but Sloan didn't think he was at any risk here and now. Not with Detective Constable Crosby answering them.

'That whoever buried Steele was a golfer?'

'Knew the course and the game,' said Sloan more precisely. There was a pause while Crosby considered the ceiling.

'Furthermore, Crosby,' Sloan tapped his notebook with his pencil, 'we must presume he was seen by old Bobby Curd the night he buried the body.'

'Sure thing, sir.'

'And knew it. Or, more sinisterly, came to know it. So he had to be killed, too.'

'One thing leading to another, you might say,' agreed Crosby.

There was an expression for this that they used in hospitals that had stuck in Sloan's mind. He quoted it aloud without thinking. 'A cascade of intervention.'

'Pardon, sir?'

'But as to why Steele was killed, Crosby, we're no further forward.'

'Someone must have a lot at stake, that's for sure, sir.'

'All right, then. Let's think about what this could be. There's the Club itself since this seems to be a golf club murder.' He looked down at his notebook. 'There's this argument about the new development for starters.'

'That's only business,' objected Crosby, leaving aside generations of slave-traders, marauding pirates and grinders down of the faces of the poor who had used much the same argument.

'Business is money,' said Sloan implacably. When it wasn't, the firm was already halfway to Carey Street.

'I've been on to the Planning people,' said Crosby with apparent irrelevance. 'They confirm that permission has been given for outline and detailed plans for all the proposed developments. No problem there.'

'That must be a first,' said Sloan sourly. 'Anything else come in?'

'Forensic say they've found lots of DNA in the greenkeeper's truck. His – that's Joe Briggs – Brian Southon's and Peter Gilchrist's – oh, and Dr Dabbe's.'

Sloan flipped back some pages in his notebook. 'Southon and Gilchrist are two of the men who cut the greens when Briggs couldn't, aren't they?'

'Yes, sir. And their fingerprints are all over the special mowers they keep for the greens, too.'

'Which is only what you'd expect,' sighed Sloan. 'You do realise, Crosby, don't you that one day soon the detective branch is going be taken over by something called deoxyribonucleic acid?'

'Sir?'

'A properly taken DNA swab can't be argued with in court.'

'Don't worry, sir,' said Crosby kindly. 'The lawyers will find a way.'

Detective Inspector Sloan acknowledged this with a quick grimace. 'All the same somewhere in the next world a Frenchman called Dr Edmond Locard must be sitting on a cloud and rubbing his hands. He was right all along.'

'What about?'

'The exchange principle, Crosby. That two matters, be they animal, vegetable or mineral, cannot meet without leaving something of themselves on each other.'

'That reminds me, sir. Mrs Sloan rang to ask if you had any idea when you would be home.'

'None,' said Sloan rather shortly. 'I'll ring her myself when I have a moment. Now, what do Forensic have to say about the golf club found in Brian Southon's bag?'

'Used with a glove and attempts made to clean it but plenty of Moffat's and some of Southon's prints on it.'

'Which is only what you would expect. And the deceased's shoes?'

'Pulled off by someone wearing gloves,' said Crosby flatly.

'Which is also only what you would expect,' sighed Sloan. 'Tell me something I wouldn't.'

'No sign of Luke Trumper's DNA or fingerprints in the greenkeeper's truck or on Moffat's club,' said the Detective Constable. 'Funny, that, isn't it?'

'Stymied, Sloan, that's what we are,' said Superintendent Leeyes.

'Very probably, sir.'

'Nothing adds up,' he complained peevishly. 'It won't do, you know.'

Detective Inspector Sloan could only agree. He could see that the game of golf meant different things to different people – exercise, a day in the country, competitive play, a sales pitch, a pathway to promotion, sociability, a good walk spoilt …but in the case of the Superintendent, it was a milieu happily far removed from his normal workaday criminal scene and thus important.

'I don't like it, Sloan,' said Leeyes. 'I come up here for pleasure, not for more work. Besides,' he added ingenuously, 'the members of the Club expect an early arrest.'

'Unless we have the figures stacked up in the wrong columns,' said Sloan, 'the only thing that makes sense so far is the murder of Bobby Curd.' He would have to get back to that crime scene as soon as he could.

'Fine lot of help that is,' declared Leeyes richly.

'And all we have to go on otherwise is a note of all the players who Steele caddied for most recently,' said Sloan. There was something else nagging at the back of his mind but he couldn't for the life of him remember what it was. Something that he must look into.

'And his friendship with the Trumper girl,' Leeyes reminded him.

'That, too,' conceded Sloan. 'There are plenty of DNA traces and fingerprint evidence about but none from anyone where we shouldn't expect them.'

Leeyes grunted.

'Someone's been very careful,' said Sloan. That much was true.

'Everything should be grist to a detective's mill,' pronounced Leeyes at his most didactic. 'Even that.'

Sloan resisted the temptation to say that it was when the

grist got to the mill that the difficulties of sorting out the wheat from the chaff showed up: especially when that grist included the facts that a suspect murder weapon had been recovered from a golf bag and a pair of the victim's shoes found in the one place where they were least likely to be noticed.

'So our murderer has got brains as well as motive, that's all,' said Leeyes racingly. 'We've got brains, too, Sloan. Remember that.' Leeyes sniffed. 'Except for Crosby. I must say he's as much use as chocolate teapot.'

'There's not even a pattern to the matches Steele caddied for,' said Sloan hastily. 'The last one seems to have been for something called the Kemberland Cup.'

'That's the three-ball Stableford I told you about,' responded Leeyes promptly. 'Played for points, not a knock-out competition. The men aren't playing against each other so they can make up their own threes just as they like.'

Detective Inspector Sloan looked down at a notebook whose pages were getting increasingly crumpled. 'Like I said, sir, Gilchrist, Trumper and Halesworth all went out together. Steele caddied for Gilchrist and Beddoes for Trumper. Halesworth carried his own clubs.'

'Too mean,' said Leeyes, adding ungraciously, 'although I suppose he is a bit younger.'

'What I would like to know,' said Sloan and not for the first time, 'is how exactly did the deceased know that Doug Garwood would beat Peter Gilchrist in the Matheson Trophy and be sure enough to bet on it.'

'I can't think,' said Leeyes irritably. 'But you'd better find out.'

Luke Trumper was in the bar. He was sitting cradling his drink at one of the tables in front of the window. Gerald Moffat and Brian Southon were with him, arguing about how Moffat's club could have been found in Southon's bag.

'I'm pretty sure it wasn't there when I was in the bunker on

Sunday morning, Gerald,' insisted Southon, frowning. 'I think I'd have noticed the thing but the trouble is I can't swear to it.'

'Was the body in the bunker then?' asked Moffat acidly. 'That's more important than whether my club was in your bag.'

'I don't know that either,' said Southon worriedly. He pushed a hand through a head of hair only just beginning to show signs of grey. 'Do I?'

Luke Trumper, older and more experienced, said 'Not your problem, that, Brian. Never does to take on something that's not your problem.'

'I suppose not,' said Southon, still looking worried, 'but all the same I don't like to think that last Sunday morning I might have been taking a stance on a dead body.'

'All bodies are dead,' said Gerald Moffat, grammarian, and even more a pedant than Edmund Pemberton.

'You know what I mean,' said Southon, flushing all the same.

Luke Trumper took a sip of his drink. 'I don't know about you two but I've just been gone over by those two detective fellows.' He pursed his lips. 'I didn't like the look in the eye of the older one. Behaved as if he didn't believe a word I said and the other behaved as if he wasn't even listening. Wanted to know when I'd last seen Matt Steele.'

'Is it true then that it's him who's dead?' asked Southon.

'They don't answer your questions,' said Luke Trumper wearily. 'They just ask theirs.'

'Such as?' said Southon.

'When Steele'd last caddied for me. I said he hadn't. Wouldn't have had him anyway even if he'd offered.' He waved an arm. 'Didn't want him talking to me about Hilary out there when I couldn't get away from him.'

'I didn't think fathers got asked for their daughter's hand in marriage any more,' murmured Moffat under his breath, 'let alone on the golf course.'

'So then they asked when I'd last gone out with anyone else who had him as a caddy,' said Trumper, without giving any sign that he'd heard Moffat.

'Which was?' asked Southon.

'Must have been the Sunday – not last Sunday. The one before. I played Peter Gilchrist in the Kemberland Cup.'

'Did you beat him?' enquired Southon.

Trumper looked up, pleased. 'Matter of fact, I did. The Steele boy caddied for Peter. Seemed all right, then.'

'He isn't all right now,' said Moffat. He jerked his shoulder in the direction of the bar. 'Molly's heard it's him so it's pretty definite.'

Once started on the Kemberland Cup Luke Trumper needed to go on. 'I had old Beddoes. Just as well we had a clear run. He'd never have heard anyone shout "fore".' He smiled reminiscently. 'It was a good match, though, in more ways than one.'

Brian Southon said to him 'Your daughter's going to be upset. I heard he was really sweet on her.'

Luke Trumper plunged his face into his glass but was heard to say 'Shouldn't speak ill of the dead, I know, but more fool her.'

'Girls will be girls,' said Gerald Moffat, bachelor and confirmed misogynist.

'I don't know if you know it, Luke,' said Brian Southon, 'but they say she's up here today.'

'Hilary?' Trumper started. 'Here? Why?'

'I don't know why, but I saw her going into the caddies' shed,' said Brian Southon, also taking refuge in his glass. 'That was after she'd left the pro's shop.'

Luke Trumper immediately pushed his glass away and quickly struggled to his feet. 'I must go and find her. Now.'

'Sorry to bother you again,' murmured Sloan to Alan Pursglove, 'but I need another look at your scoresheets.'

'No trouble,' said the Secretary amiably. 'They're all up on the board over there.'

'You kick off your season with the Clarembald Cup, don't you?' Sloan turned. 'Make a note of that, Crosby, will you?'

'It's the first of our major Club competitions,' agreed Pursglove. He added in deadpan tones 'And as you can see from the chart your Superintendent Leeyes got knocked out very early on.'

'There's no need to write that down, Crosby,' said Sloan.

'No, sir.'

'Both Doug Garwood and Peter Gilchrist had got as far as the third round.' Pursglove grinned. 'The third round's usually the one to sort out the men from the boys.'

In the police force it was usually night duty that sorted out the men from the boys. And sometimes the girls from both.

'You can see that Doug beat Peter Gilchrist and went on to play in the semi-final.' The Secretary ran his finger along the score sheet. 'He didn't win that round, though. He met a real tiger coming up the other leg and got knocked out.'

'Then?'

'Then there's the Pletchford Plate. Everyone was meant to have played their second round of that by the end of last week.' Pursglove moved along the wall to another chart. 'They're at quarter-final level now. Major Bligh had to play James Hopland and it was Peter Gilchrist versus Brian Southon. Brian was lucky there because he'd had a walkover from Eric Simmonds in the previous round. He's been ill, Simmonds, I mean, and couldn't play. Some sort of tummy trouble.'

'Make a note of all this, Crosby,' he said quietly. So it was Simmonds whose name he had been trying to remember as having been taken ill as well as Joe Briggs, the greenkeeper. He didn't know whether this fact was wheat or chaff but he would soon find out.

'Leeyes lost his match in that, too,' said Pursglove, straight-faced.

'Forget that as well, Crosby,' said Sloan.

'Yes, sir.'

'And then there's the Kemberland Cup,' said Alan Pursglove. 'It's a Stableford Competition. That's nowhere near finished yet but it was the last match Matt Steele caddied for before he...'

'Quite,' said Detective Inspector Sloan. 'Quite.'

'How did the Superintendent do in that one?' asked Crosby with an air of innocence.

Pursglove consulted the score sheet. 'Twenty-three points.'

'Is that good?' enquired the Constable.

'Well below average,' said the Secretary.

Crosby gently closed his notebook, his face suffused with a seraphic smile. 'Fancy that,' he said.

'Just suppose, Crosby,' said Sloan, sitting back in his chair, 'that the illness of Eric Simmonds is as important as the illness of the greenkeeper.'

'Who?' asked the Constable. Alan Pursglove had left the two policemen on their own in his room. The Detective Constable was standing at the window watching a foursome working its way towards the eighteenth green.

'Eric Simmonds. The man who was taken ill and so had to concede his match to Brian Southon.' The operative word was "taken": it might be too late now to prove that a noxious substance had been involved.

'How could that be important?' asked Crosby.

'His illness could have been engineered so that Peter

Gilchrist could play against Brian Southon.'

'Or Southon against Gilchrist,' said Crosby idly.

'That, too. I wonder...' Detective Inspector Sloan stopped and stared unseeingly at the various oddments on the Secretary's desk. 'Gilchrist played against Garwood first and then against Southon and the deceased caddied for both matches.'

'Nothing odd about that,' said Crosby, his attention still held by the players on the eighteenth fairway.

'Southon works for Garwood, doesn't he? And doing well from all accounts.'

The Data Protection Acts never stopped anyone from asking around.

'His number two,' said Crosby laconically.

'What could make it important that Gilchrist played Southon?'

'Or the other way round,' persisted Crosby without turning his gaze away from the window.

'And what, if anything, could Steele have overheard when caddying for Garwood against Gilchrist that mattered?'

Displaying manifest disinterest, Crosby announced that one of the men playing the eighteenth had hit his ball into the wood.

'Then he'll have to hit it out again, won't he?' said Sloan unsympathetically.

Detection was a more difficult game than golf. Detection was an uneasy marriage of logic and evidence. And at the moment they were rather short of both. What golf was a marriage of, he wasn't sure. Character and luck, probably.

'He's having a go,' reported Crosby.

'Bully for him.'

'Oh, look, another of them's gone into a bunker.'

'Whatever it was that Steele overheard,' declared Sloan insistently, 'it must have told him that Gilchrist would lose to Garwood in the Matheson Trophy.'

'So Gilchrist owed Garwood,' concluded Crosby with elegant simplicity. 'Oh, good, that man's out of the wood.'

'Which is more than we are,' Sloan came back with some asperity. 'You do realise, Crosby, don't you, that Matthew Steele must have known it whatever it was.'

'Or guessed,' said Crosby.

'Or guessed. But that's what mattered.'

'Yes, sir,' said Crosby. 'Much good it did him if it led to him ending up in the bunker on the sixth.'

'But you're with me so far, I take it?' said Sloan with elaborate politeness.

'Steele wasn't the only caddy, sir.'

'Ah, he was the first time. The second time the other caddy was the man they call Belloes. The deaf man.'

'Doesn't get us very far though, sir, does it?' So far the Detective Constable hadn't taken his gaze off the fairway.

Detective Inspector Sloan tilted his chair back. Somewhere at the back of his mind an elusive thought was teasing him. There was a famous precedent, surely, for a man exacting something on behalf of his employer and coming to grief in the process. He ran his mind rapidly through such case law as he could remember but answer came there none.

'They're on the green now,' reported Crosby.

Only it wasn't the servant of Calleshire Consolidated – Brian Southon in this case – who had come to grief but a bystander who might – or might not – have been innocent.

Whilst the game of golf meant different things to different players, to the most of the caddies it usually spelt one thing – money.

'Might as well go home,' said Dickie Castle, although making no move to leave.

'Nothing more doing here today,' agreed Bert Hedges, nevertheless continuing to stand in front of the window. 'And if you was hoping for a round today, young Ginger, you'll just have to go on hoping, that's all. Anyone who's going out today's gone out already notwithstanding the sixth being what you might call ground under repair.'

'If you say so,' said Edmund Pemberton, making no move to go either. 'I do wish Hilary had let me take her home, though. It's a bit worrying.'

'She wasn't going home, remember,' said Dickie Castle. 'Not never.'

'Sounded as she meant it, too,' put in Bert Hedges. He sniffed. 'You can always tell when a woman means what she says.'

'There wasn't any "stop it, I like it" about her,' agreed Castle sagely.

'If she wasn't going home, then where was she going?' asked Edmund Pemberton anxiously.

'Don't ask me, lad,' said Castle. 'Wherever it was she wasn't telling me or you or anyone else.'

'Mr Bigboots might know,' suggested Bert Hedges.

'The Captain, you mean?' asked Pemberton innocently.

Castle gave a humourless laugh. 'No, not him. I mean Mr Almighty Jock Selkirk, the professional. He thinks he knows everything about the game that there is to know.'

'And the course,' chimed in Hedges.

'And does he?' asked Pemberton, looking bewildered.

'Course he doesn't,' said Castle richly.

'Not even the half of it,' said Hedges.

'But what is there to know?' Pemberton might be young and innocent but he wasn't stupid.

'Like somewhere Hilary might have gone,' said Hedges, sucking his teeth. 'Like someone Bobby Curd might have seen.'

'More like someone she might have gone to,' chimed in Castle. 'Seeing as she's fallen out with her father like she has.'

He suddenly turned away from the window. 'Look out, men. Here comes trouble in trousers.'

Police Sergeant Polly Perkins slipped inside the caddies' shed and said without any usual womanly preamble 'I'm looking for Hilary Trumper. Anyone here know where I'll find her?'

There was a united shaking of heads followed by a silence that no one man seemed to want to broach. This was clearly a situation that Sergeant Perkins had met before. Many times. 'All right then,' she said. 'Tell me someone else who might know.'

'You could try the professional, miss, – I mean, madam,' offered Hedges promptly.

'Right,' she said, taking a quick look round the assembled men, 'but before I go, tell me when any of you last saw a Mr Robert Curd up here.'

Achieving a concensus of opinion among the caddies on this took time but the general feeling was that it would have been at the weekend.

'I think I saw him trying to sell the professional some old balls on Saturday morning,' offered one caddy cautiously, 'but then I might not have done.'

'For repainting,' said another.

'And for using as practice balls,' said Dickie Castle. 'He does it most weekends.'

'With those he's picked up the Sunday before,' expanded someone else.

'But if you'd really wanted to catch him after that,' said Bert Hedges, 'you'd have had to have been around up here after dark.'

'Someone was,' said Sergeant Perkins briefly. 'Now, where will I find the professional?'

Eager hands pointed her in the direction of the man's shop.

'Right,' she said.

By the time the policewoman got there it was locked and empty.

'Hullo, there, Hilary,' called out the man who was walking across the car park as a disconsolate Hilary Trumper stumbled across the forecourt. 'I'm just going home. Can I give you a lift anywhere?'

'Oh, please,' said Hilary eagerly. 'Would you?'

'Hop in,' he said, opening the passenger door for her. 'Where to?'

'Anywhere,' she said, dropping down on the seat.

'Home?'

'Anywhere except home,' she said tightly.

'Problems?' He started up the engine and engaged first gear.

'Big problems.' Suddenly Hilary ducked her head down well below the windscreen. 'Can you get a move on, please? Dad's just come out of the Clubhouse and I don't want him to see me.'

'Like that, is it?' He gave her a sympathetic grin. 'Happens to us all sometimes.' He steered the car out onto the open road and then said 'It's all right. You can sit up again now. He's gone off towards the caddies' shed.'

'Much good that'll do him,' said Hilary grimly.

'If it's not home you want to go to, Hilary, then where is it?'

'What I should really like,' Hilary Trumper said with unusual docility, 'is to go to my grandmother's.'

'Ah, yes, of course. I understand.'

'So does she,' said the girl. 'Granny knows everything.' She hesitated. 'It's not too far for you, is it?'

'Of course not. She lives out Larking way, doesn't she?'

'That's right but you could drop me anywhere on the way.'

'No trouble at all,' he said affably. 'I've just got to make one call on a chap on my way, if that's all right with you? Bit of unfinished business, you might say.'

'That's fine with me,' she said, settling back comfortably in the front passenger seat. Presently she said 'Look here, I'm not taking you out of your way, am I?'

'Not at all.'

A little later still she said 'You're quite sure this isn't putting you out at all?'

'Quite sure,' he said urbanely. 'I've been quite looking forward to having a little chat with you on my own and now's my chance.'

'The doctor couldn't put his finger on Eric's trouble,' said Mrs Simmonds. 'Thought he must have eaten something but he was really ill for a while.' She patted a cretonne-covered chair. 'Take a seat, Inspector.' She looked anxiously at Detective Constable Crosby. 'Will you be all right on the pouffe?'

'That's the sort of stool over there, Crosby,' intervened Sloan quickly. 'The velvet one.'

Crosby nodded as he tried to perch on the distinctly unstable stuffed seat. Having failed to straddle it, he settled for a form of uncomfortable side-saddle.

'Eric's only just stepped outside for a little walk. He'll be back presently because he's not quite up to going far yet but I expect I can help you. He tells me all about the Club after he's played.'

Detective Inspector Sloan projected sympathy and interest.

'He didn't even feel like going to the Committee meeting today, you know. Anyway,' she said placidly, 'he said there would be bound to be argument and Eric certainly wasn't up to that.'

Sloan said that in his experience you had to be fit and well to attend any Committee meeting.

'Just what I said to Eric.' Her face brightened. 'Besides, he doesn't really want to have to decide who is going to get to do all the new work they want doing there. He said that they're all old friends up there and it wasn't right that he should have to choose between them.'

'I expect they'll take the cheapest estimate,' said Sloan. The Calleshire Police Committee always did. And paid for it very heavily in the long run.

'I suppose so,' she said doubtfully. 'Never mind, I said to him, you'll soon be back playing and that's more important than any old Committee meeting.'

'Much,' said Sloan heartily. It wasn't his duty to tell her that they weren't all friends at the Golf Club. On the contrary, in fact: some of them at the very least were rival contenders for its business. And one of them had murdered twice. And probably fed mild poison to two more...

'Mind you, Inspector, Eric was very sorry to miss some of the competitions. Especially the Pletchford Plate.' She pointed to a great salver adorning the mantelpiece. 'He won that last year and now it'll have to go back for someone else to have.'

'Got to give the others a chance,' said Crosby, struggling to keep his balance.

'And he did so well in the first rounds,' she said, ignoring this sportsman-like sentiment. 'He was ever so disappointed that he had to give Brian Southon a walkover because he was looking forward to playing him. He'd have beaten him, too, I'm sure.'

'Would he?' asked Sloan, uncertain still whether he was dealing with wheat or chaff.

'Eric's a much steadier player than Mr Southon,' she said proudly. 'And he was on top form. Do you know he had three horseshoes in the last match he played before he was ill and still won?'

Sloan confessed to an ignorance of golfing horseshoes.

'It's when the ball runs round the rim of the hole and doesn't drop in,' she informed him. 'Hard, isn't it?'

'Nerve-racking,' said Sloan.

'"Never up, never in", is what Eric always says,' said Mrs Simmonds.

'It's what they all say,' muttered Crosby, *sotto voce*.

For a fleeting moment Sloan wondered how much his wife quoted him on rose-growing over the garden fence. He hoped not. What he had to say on white-fly ought not to be repeated in company.

'Assuming he'd beaten Brian Southon,' said Detective Inspector Sloan casually, 'he'd have had to go on and beat quite a few other men to win in the end.'

'Oh, yes, I know,' she said, more golf wife than golf widow. 'Peter Gilchrist, first, of course.' She smiled. 'Now that was one good thing to come out of Eric's illness although naturally he didn't see it that way.'

'What was?' asked Sloan on the instant.

'Eric told me that Brian Southon had been trying ever so hard to fix up a game with Peter Gilchrist but that Peter hadn't got any spare dates at all.'

'Well, I never,' said Crosby.

'So they were able to get together after all in the Pletchford Plate.' She beamed. 'I always think that things work out for the best in the long run, don't you, Inspector?'

'Sometimes,' said Sloan, getting to his feet. 'But not always for everyone. Come along, Crosby.'

'What Eric really wants to do one day,' said Mrs Simmonds happily, 'is to shoot his age. But I'm sure he'll answer all your questions himself when he comes in. Oh, you're going now, are you? Don't you want to wait and see him? He'll be so disappointed to have missed you.'

The radio in the police car came to life as soon as the two policemen stepped back inside it.

'Inspector Sloan? Sergeant Perkins here.' There was the sound of distant background noises contributing to the crackling over the airwaves betokening a call being made in the open air. 'I couldn't find Hilary Trumper anywhere at the Golf Club. Not anywhere but...'

'Put out a general call,' interrupted Sloan without hesitation. 'If seen, stop and detain for questioning.'

'But Molly from the bar saw her get into someone's car about five minutes ago. I'm sorry but she doesn't know whose.' Sergeant Perkins sounded apologetic on behalf of her sex. 'She's very sorry but she's not into cars and she doesn't know which car belongs to which member.'

'And make a note of everyone who is still at the Club,' said Sloan automatically. Not even a golfer had solved the problem of being in two places at once.

'Her father's still there,' said Polly Perkins.

'That's something.'

'But the professional isn't.'

'Noted.'

'Then they drove off,' went on the policewoman, 'without Molly being able to see who was driving. All she knows is that the car took the Calleford road but of course that could mean anything.'

'He could have taken a turning to anywhere he wanted at the Billing cross-roads,' agreed Sloan, the map of the county's road network as clear in his mind as it was on paper. 'It's only half a mile down that road.'

She hesitated. 'Quite a lot of the men had already started to drift away after they'd finished playing so in theory it could be anyone who isn't still there.'

'We're on our way,' said Sloan, giving his driver a nod. 'All right, Crosby, you can get going now.'

'Where to, sir?'

'Good question.' He pulled out his notebook. 'Back to the Golf Club first while I try to work out why it could be so important for Brian Southon to be able to have a nice quiet round with Peter Gilchrist...'

'Or Peter Gilchrist with Brian Southon.'

'No, Crosby. That wasn't what Mrs Simmonds said. Weren't you listening?'

'That round thing was very difficult to sit on, sir.'

'Well listen now. Suppose it was important that instead of Eric Simmonds playing Gilchrist that Southon played in his place – important enough for Southon to have made Simmonds ill.'

'If he did.'

'We don't know that yet.' Doctors and ordinary pathologists would have to be consulted, he knew, before anyone – especially the lawyers – could be sure about that. 'But why?'

'Blackmail?' suggested Crosby, letting in the clutch.

'They don't call it that any more, Crosby,' said Sloan. 'It's "Biographical leverage" if you don't mind.'

'That then.'

'No.' He considered this for a long moment. 'You can apply that sort of pressure at any time anywhere. No, I think this encounter was meant to appear more casual. Better than making an appointment to see him or anything like that.'

'Why?' asked Crosby.

'There you have me…' Sloan stared unseeingly at his notebook.

'Something Steele heard and understood, though,' suggested Crosby intelligently.

'I think so. And perhaps something that Steele could have put together with something else,' reasoned Sloan, 'because neither Gilchrist nor Southon is silly enough to have said anything patently obvious in front of a caddy.'

'Put two and two together, did he, sir?' said Crosby, pulling the car out of Eric Simmonds' drive and onto the road.

'And made five?'

'And made four, I'm afraid,' said Sloan. 'That would have been the trouble.'

The Constable gave a prodigious frown. 'Gilchrist and Steele were both together, too, when Steele caddied for Southon's boss, Doug Garwood, in his match with Peter Gilchrist,' said Crosby. 'That was earlier, of course.'

The effect of this on Detective Inspector Sloan was remarkable. He slapped his notebook down on his knee and said softly. 'Of course! I knew it had happened before but I couldn't remember.'

'What had?' asked Crosby. 'When?'

'To Elisha and Naaman and Gehazi. And as to when, it was a very long time ago.' He leaned forward and spoke into the car's microphone. 'Get me the registration number of any vehicle belonging to Brian Southon of Berebury and order all cars to search. Utmost urgency. May be off the road by now...'

'But who were they?' asked Crosby.

'Garwood was Elisha, Gilchrist was Naaman and Southon was Gehazi. Don't you see? Gehazi was Elisha's servant, which was the whole trouble.'

Detective Constable Crosby, servant of the State, did not see. Instead he switched on the police car's blue light and stepped up his speed. This was something he did understand.

'It wasn't Gilchrist who wanted to play with Southon, then,' said Sloan, 'it was Southon who wanted to play with Gilchrist.'

The car wasn't off the road.

Not yet.

But it was heading that way.

'So Matt talked to you about the Club a lot, did he?' asked Brian Southon.

'A bit,' admitted Hilary Trumper nervously. She shot him a sideways glance and said hastily 'Not a lot.'

'Thought so,' said Southon with quiet satisfaction. 'Otherwise you'd never have come snooping around like you did after you thought he'd gone away. Asked you to keep an eye open, I expect. Well, didn't he?'

'He might have done,' she said.

'What have you told the police?'

'Nothing,' she said. 'They were looking for me but I cleared off...'

'Good.' He smiled abstractedly. 'That's what I thought.'

'Look here, this isn't the way out to Larking.'

'Isn't it?' He twisted his lips. 'Well, it's the way we're going.'

'We're going south,' she said.

'Little Miss Clever.' He tightened his grip on the steering wheel. 'I told you I had a call to make on the way first.'

'Larking's the other way.'

'So it may be,' he said smoothly, 'but we're not going to Larking.'

'Then you can put me out here and I'll find my own way to Granny's,' she said with youthful dignity.

'Oh, no, I can't,' he said, leaning back in the driving seat. 'Not now.'

'What do you mean?' The girl reached over and started to unfasten her seat belt.

'I mean that I can't let you out of the car at all.'

'Why not?'

'Because of what that little rat, Matt, told you, that's why.'

'Matthew wasn't a rat,' she said tearfully.

'That's where you're wrong,' Southon said smoothly. 'Very wrong.'

'He was just against people doing the wrong thing,' she sobbed.

'Only if he couldn't cut himself into the action,' said Southon harshly. 'He tried his funny tricks on me and nobody who does that gets away with it.' His voice hardened. 'Nobody, do you understand? Nobody at all.'

'I understand,' she said in a small voice. 'Now, stop the car and let me out.'

'No way.'

'They were doing something wrong...' she stopped suddenly, her hand over her mouth, colour draining away from her face.

'Ah, then he did tell you all,' he said with a certain perverse satisfaction. 'I thought so.' He put his foot down on the accelerator. 'That settles it.'

Chapter Nineteen

'All roads leading from the Billing crossroads,' barked Detective Inspector Sloan into the microphone. 'We need roadblocks on the four of them. Urgently. He could have gone anything up to twelve miles by now.'

'And turned off anywhere,' muttered Crosby. He was itching to go somewhere fast but at the moment there was nowhere to go fast. Instead he was following fresh orders and proceeding – by driving, against all his instincts, at a sedate pace, back in the direction the Golf Club.

'True.' Sloan sank back in the passenger seat, thinking hard. 'They're checking that the girl hasn't just gone home or to any friends or family.'

Detective Constable Crosby didn't really care whether chases were wild goose ones or not.

'And that he hasn't already dropped her off somewhere and just gone home.'

Presumptions of innocence didn't appeal to Crosby either.

'What we have to do,' said Sloan, half-aloud, 'is to work out where a man would take a girl if he wanted to do away with her quietly.'

'Me, sir? I'd stage a hit and run,' said Crosby. 'All you need is a narrow road between high banks. And no witnesses, of course.'

This revealing train of thought was interrupted by another crackle from the microphone.

'Vehicle in question seen travelling through Little Barling village,' reported an unknown voice. 'Going in a southward direction.'

Crosby had braked and already half-turned the police car before the message ended.

'Find and keep in view,' ordered Sloan. 'Do not approach.'

A man who had killed twice wasn't going to balk at a third time.

The microphone crackled back. 'Understood. We've got two vehicles coming north to meet him head-on if he's still on that road.'

'Block it before the first turn-off,' commanded Sloan.

'I bet he's heading for the woods,' said Crosby, completing the about-turn and running up through the gears.

'Then so are we,' said Sloan. 'Get moving, Crosby. It doesn't do to hang about at a time like this.'

'That you, Margaret? Chris here.' He heard the coins drop down in the payphone as he rang home. 'I'm nearly on my way.'

'Is that a promise?' she enquired sweetly.

'Sort of,' he said.

'Just a few loose ends?' she suggested with fine irony.

'In a manner of speaking, yes.'

'Do you think you'll make a player?'

'Give me roses,' he said fervently. 'Any day.'

'No need to be like that,' she said, patently disappointed.

'Listen love, I've got to go back to the Golf Club first…'

'Go back? Where are you then?'

'The hospital,' he said awkwardly.

'The hospital? Chris, what's happened? You're not hurt, are you?'

'Not really.'

'And what exactly is that supposed to mean?' she demanded fiercely. 'Tell me… quickly…no messing about, now.'

'We had a little run-in with a villain, that's all. Nothing to worry about.'

'Nothing to worry about?' she echoed on a rising note. 'What happened?'

'Crosby floored it and rammed a guy we were chasing.

Didn't do the car a lot of good and Crosby's got the mother and father of black eyes. We got him,' he added.

'And you?' she said, dismissing captured villains as irrelevant.

'Nothing serious.'

'That's not an answer.'

'Bruised.'

'Where?'

'Everywhere,' he said. 'He had the girl in the car, you see…' That was paramount.

'What girl?'

'Tell you later,' he said, suddenly very tired. 'Crosby caught it though when the guy tripped him up. He was making for the woods south of Little Barling. The girl wouldn't have stood a chance if he'd got there without anyone knowing.'

Margaret Sloan shuddered. 'But he put up a fight?'

'I'll say.' He brightened. 'So did Crosby.'

She sighed. 'You'd better bring him back with you.'

'I've got to see the Super first and then we'll be on our way.' He hesitated and then said, 'And that is a promise.'

'I still don't get it, Sloan.' The Superintendent was sitting on one of the wooden seats outside the Clubhouse, one eye on his subordinate, the other on a foursome playing the eighteenth hole.

'None of them appreciated that the deceased was a student of business studies and economics,' said Sloan.

'Come to that, neither did I,' said Leeyes frankly, 'but what's it got to do with his being murdered?'

'Everything, sir,' said Sloan. 'Most people overhearing what he did wouldn't have understood its significance.'

'Its significance was what I don't understand,' grumbled Leeyes with some asperity. He said at his most Churchillian, 'Pray explain…'

'The trouble started when Gilchrist played Doug Garwood...'

'I don't know about Gilchrist,' interrupted Leeyes, 'but I would have sworn Doug Garwood was as straight as a die.'

'I'm sure he is,' said Sloan. 'But Peter Gilchrist is only half straight.'

'Crooked,' said Leeyes succinctly.

'Up to a point,' agreed Sloan. 'But not to the point of murder.'

'Sloan, I am not prepared to sit here all afternoon and...'

'What Gilchrist urgently needed to know from Garwood,' said Sloan hastily, 'was whether or not his company Calleshire Consolidated was going to tender for the development work at the Golf Club.'

'Go on.'

'Garwood almost certainly told Gilchrist privately that they weren't. He didn't have to, of course, but I think he did.'

'It would have been like him. So?'

'So Gilchrist could then go ahead and fix the price of the tender with his two pals, Luke Trumper of Trumper and Trumper (Berebury) Ltd., and Nigel Halesworth of United Mellemetics. Probably on the usual understanding that he would divvy the profit with them afterwards. Remember, his firm was known to be short of work anyway so in that sort of set-up he'd naturally be the one to get it.'

'Bid rigging,' divined Leeyes on the instant. 'That's what that's called.'

'Definitely against the law,' agreed Sloan tacitly.

'So that's why Matt Steele could be so sure that Peter Gilchrist would let Doug Garwood win the Matheson Trophy,' snorted Leeyes.

'Well, sir, he's not going to beat Garwood, is he? Not when he owes the man a favour. And it's easy enough to lose your own ball.'

Leeyes still sounded dissatisfied. 'I don't see where murder comes in to this,'

'It didn't until Steele also caddied for a match between Gilchrist and Brian Southon, a match that Southon arranged by making sure that Eric Simmonds was ill enough to have to give him a walkover.'

'And?'

'Matt Steele caddies for that match, too, with old Beddoes.'

'Who still doesn't hear a thing.'

'Matt Steele does, though,' said Sloan warmly. 'He hears Southon, who you know is Garwood's number two at Calleshire Consolidated, make up some cock-and-bull tale and informally suggest a bit of recompense on Doug's behalf for Doug having given Gilchrist the info.'

'Opportunity makes the thief,' said Leeyes sagaciously.

'You can imagine how he put it – valuable commercial information, Doug not liking to ask himself, and all that guff.'

'I can,' said Leeyes grimly.

'Brian Southon probably extracts some reward from Gilchrist either in cash or in the shape of favourable treatment from Gilchrist's firm at the expense of his usual suppliers. The sort of thing that'll do him a bit of good with Doug, perhaps.'

'Business is business,' said Leeyes ineluctably.

'What Southon didn't know,' said Sloan, leaving this pagan sentiment aside for the time being, 'is that Matt was present both times and put two and two together.'

'What they both forgot,' said Leeyes grandly, 'was *pas devant les domestiques.*'

'Pardon, sir?'

'It's how the French warn you about loose talk. They say "not in front of the servants".'

'Quite so, sir.' That must have come from the winter of the Superintendent's "French Without Tears" evening class. 'Very wise of the French.' Sloan coughed and, trying not to sound sanctimonious, changed tack. 'And what neither of them had studied, sir, was the Old Testament.' He had his Mother's Bible Class to thank for this. Her Sunday lunchtime mantra was that the Bible was better than any of his text-books on crime.

Superintendent Leeyes rose suddenly to his feet, pointed and said 'Look out. That shot's going to be out of bounds.'

'The Second Book of Kings,' Sloan persisted. 'I understand it was forbidden to have it read aloud in monasteries at meal-times on account of its being too exciting.' That came from his Mother's Bible Class, too.

'Sloan, if I find you've been having me on...'

'Chapter Five,' said Sloan. 'Elisha wouldn't accept anything for the good turn he did Naaman but Elisha's servant Gehazi had overheard all and tried to get something out of Naaman all the same.'

'I still don't see why...'

'I think that's when Matt would have thought it would be a good idea to put the screws on Brian Southon for acting like – er – Gehazi.' He hesitated. 'And cut himself into the action, so to speak.'

'Big, big mistake,' pronounced Leeyes. 'Southon wouldn't have stood for that. Couldn't have. Besides, once you pay dane-geld you never get rid of the Dane.'

Detective Inspector Sloan placed that quotation without difficulty. It had come straight from the evening class "Kipling – A Man For All Time", when for at least two weeks the Superintendent had tried to treat those twin impostors "Triumph and Disaster" just the same.

And failed.

'It seems that Steele was a bit of a chancer anyway,' said Sloan. 'Out for what he could get, girlfriend included.'

'Doug Garwood wouldn't have stood for anything that wasn't hunky-dory,' declared Leeyes, 'that's for sure.'

'Southon's got much too much to lose by then. He'd be
out on his ear if Steele split on him to Garwood, and he could-
n't have afforded that. Not with a wife into antique silver.
Besides…'

'Besides what?'

'Besides that's not all, sir.'

'Go on,' said Leeyes gruffly.

'Steele was also present when the three contenders for the
development work played with each other. They'd all chosen
to enter the Kemberland Cup together.'

'Good communication in a natural setting is what you need
when you're setting up a cartel,' declared Leeyes authorita-
tively. 'And no records.'

'Something that Crosby said brought it to mind.'

'Crosby? Are you sure?'

'He drew my attention to the fact that when you kicked
one of them, they all limped.'

Detective Inspector Sloan gazed down the eighteenth hole,
a recission of the many shades of green, and thought about
Gilchrist, Trumper and Halesworth all playing together under
an English heaven so that they could rip off their own Club.

'Any sector where there are very few competitors is vulnerable to an agreement in restraint of trade,' said Leeyes horta-
tively. 'The Club made a big mistake in wanting to keep the
work in-house.'

'Those three wouldn't have taken any notice of Matt Steele
overhearing them either because they hadn't cottoned on to
his being such a bright cookie. They didn't know their chat
would have been right up his street seeing as he was reading
business studies and economics and had heard Doug Garwood
being asked into the bargain.'

'And where does the girl Hilary Trumper come in?' asked
Leeyes, his eyes still on the fairway in front of him. A working life-time with police estimates had left him still unable to

distinguish between economy and economics and he automatically shied away from both words.

'She says that Matt passed some of his suspicions about the cartel on to her.'

'She's all right, you say?'

'Shaken to her little wattles,' said Sloan, 'and bruised where he'd got his hands round her throat but alive all right.'

Leeyes grunted.

'Matt asked her to keep an eye open while he was away, that's all. He didn't mention Southon's involvment to her. She says she'd never have got into his car if he had.'

'I do wish people would leave police work to the police,' said the Superintendent pettishly.

Sloan coughed 'If the girl's father were implicated, then I wouldn't have been surprised if Matt planned to demand his own terms for the marriage when he got back. Like an early seat on the Board.'

'Far-sighted lad,' commented Leeyes sardonically. 'Mind you, marrying the boss's daughter never did a man any harm.'

'I think she's had a lucky escape, sir.' He paused. 'She doesn't think so yet but she will – given time.'

Leeyes came as near as he ever did to awarding an accolade. 'Just as well you got there in time,' he said.

'Only just,' said Sloan truthfully. 'It was a near thing and I don't like to think what would have happened if Crosby had been any slower.'

'And I,' said Superintendent Leeyes pointedly, 'don't like to think what will happen if he gets any faster.'

Gerald Moffat was still sitting in the Clubhouse in front of the picture windows that gave out onto the course. With him were Major Bligh and James Hopland.

'I don't think we should have put that fellow Leeyes in charge of the flagpole,' said Major Bligh. 'He doesn't know the first thing about it. Look, it's practically sunset and they're only just hoisting the Club standard. It's all wrong.'

'I can tell you he'll never make a vexillologist,' snorted Moffat, ever the schoolmaster. 'The man doesn't even know that half-mast doesn't literally mean halfway down the mast.'

'What does it mean, then?' asked James Hopland.

'Half-mast means that it's been lowered just enough to take another flag on top, that's all,' said Moffat. 'The flag of the new head of the family should fly just over the flag of the man whom you've just lost. It should only be lowered enough to take the new one. No more.'

'The king is dead, long live the king,' remarked Bligh.

'He should have left it to Arthur,' said James Hopland.

'I said to Leeyes that we haven't lost a member anyway,' said Major Bligh. He looked at the other two. 'Do you know what he said?'

'Tell us?' invited Hopland.

'He said we'd lost four members.'

'Four?'

'One to prison and three who would have to resign for offences against some Act or other making cartels illegal.'

'We may have lost them but not to death,' said Moffat, a stickler if ever there was one. 'That's what flags are all about.'

'Then there's the boy Steele and old Bobby Curd,' said Hopland. 'They did die. What about them?'

Major Bligh said quietly. 'I think we'll just take it that it's been lowered for them.' He sighed. 'Easier than trying to tell Leeyes anything, don't you think?'

'It'll do the Major a bit of good, though,' said Dickie Castle comfortably, 'all those other men not being there. Gilchrist would have been bound to have knocked him out in the next round of the Pletchford and now he won't.'

'I reckon old James Hopland'll be in with a chance in the

Matheson Trophy now,' said Bert Hedges. 'Since all those younger players will be out of the way.'

Shipley scratched his chin. 'Don't forget Doug Garwood.'

Bert Hedges grinned. 'Doug? He'll be much too busy supervising the new work to play golf.'

'I thought,' stumbled Edmund Pemberton, 'that he didn't want the job.'

Bert Hedges looked cunning. 'He doesn't.'

'That makes him the best person to give it to,' explained Dickie Castle. 'Can't you see that, young Ginger?'

Edmund Pemberton had no answer to this and shook his head.

'By the way, young Ginger,' said Bert Hedges magnanimously, 'we've lined up someone for you to caddy for tomorrow.'

The boy's head came up eagerly.

'That's right,' said Dickie Castle. 'A man called Moffat. Gerald Moffat. Slow but sure.'

'Very sure,' said Hedges. 'And, young Ginger...'

'Yes?'

'If anyone you're caddying for loses his ball in The Gulf Stream, just let us know. No going in after it yourself. That understood?'

Edmund Pemberton nodded.

'Another thing,' said Bert Castle. 'Don't let Mr Moffat leave his number nine-iron anywhere on the course, that's all.'

'I ought to have tumbled to Southon sooner,' said Detective Inspector Sloan.

He was back in Alan Pursglove's office at the Golf Club on the Saturday morning with Detective Constable Crosby. They were not so much catching up on the paperwork as taking it down from the walls to be used in evidence.

'I don't see how...' began Crosby. He was still sporting

two black eyes collected from a muscular Southon.

'Because he'd taken such very good care to make sure that there were reasons for either his fingerprints or his DNA being in all of the suspicious places,' said Sloan. 'He'd used the greenkeeper's truck to help cut the greens as well as to carry the body out to the bunker.'

'And told us so,' agreed the Detective Constable. 'Early on.'

'Gerald Moffat's club was found in his bag, don't forget,' said Sloan. 'He probably took it that day they played together and it's the one that killed Curd, too. Forensic say so.'

'So it must be true,' said Crosby. 'Mustn't it?'

'Best of all,' said Sloan, ignoring this, 'he played a ball into the bunker at the sixth on the Sunday.'

'Never up, never in,' chanted Crosby.

'So if his footprints had been found there,' said Sloan ignoring this, too, 'they could be explained. And he went to see the professional for advice on shanking to make sure everyone knew about it.'

The door of the room opened and a woman's head came round. 'Ah, there you are,' said Sergeant Perkins. 'Molly said to try in here. There's some food to come, you'll be glad to hear.'

'Good,' said Crosby.

'You may not like it but it's all they had at this time of the day.'

'Better than nothing,' said Crosby.

'They call it "Yips",' said the policewoman, 'but it looks like pork scratchings to me.'

'Hilary Trumper?' began Sloan.

'More glad to get back home than she ever thought she would be,' said Sergeant Perkins, who had restored a good few youngsters to their official dwelling-places in her time. 'And as soon as the trial's safely over Granny's taking her away for a long holiday. Round the world cruise or something.'

'Good for Granny.'

'They don't want her around when the commercial case comes up,' explained Sergeant Perkins. 'Or Granny, come to that,' she added, having now met that formidable matriarch.

'I'm not surprised,' said Sloan, having met her too. 'I gather she is not pleased with her sons.'

'That's an understatement. How are you getting on here?' asked Polly Perkins.

'You could say,' said Sloan deftly, 'that we're making space on the wall for an election notice for the Committee.'

'Ah...' She grinned.

'Voting's next week,' said Crosby. 'Never up, never in,' he added inconsequentially.

Polly Perkins went over to look. 'Rupert Almeric Leeyes? I never knew he was called Rupert Almeric.'

'You do now.' Sloan sat back. 'Then, thank goodness, I think we can shake the dust of the place off our feet.'

Sergeant Perkins looked unusually bashful. 'Not quite,' she said. 'The Lady Captain thinks I ought to join. She says I've got just the figure for the game and she'll put me up.'

'Never up, never in,' said Crosby again.